Sutton had completed his years of Service and was now a wealthy independent marked man. The only thing he was missing was someone to share his life with—someone who sexually dominated him like he craved. He met Gray Carron, the young recently-appointed US Ambassador to Romania. He felt a pull towards Gray that was unlike any he had ever felt before. Sutton accepts his invitation to come to Romania to be with him. Romania doesn't turn out to be the paradise that Gray promised and Sutton is experiencing some strange physical symptoms. He is hounded by a local gang who brings him before their leader. The Pack Master is unlike any man Sutton has even fantasized about. Together they seek answers to questions that are only found when Sutton gives up total control to the Master.

The Pack Master
Copyright © 2019 Crawford Rhine
ISBN: 978-1-4874-1604-1
Cover art by Angela Waters

Published by eXtasy Books Inc or
Devine Destinies, an imprint of eXtasy Books Inc

Look for us online at:
www.eXtasybooks.com or www.devinedestinies.com

THE PACK MASTER
ROMANIAN CHRONICLES BOOK 3

BY

CRAWFORD RHINE

CHAPTER ONE

Text string between Sutton Pike and Preston Sway, April 21, 2015:

Are you back in town, Sutton?
I am. Just off the plane!
How were the Seychelles?
Fabulous! I'm completely tan and relaxed . . .
Find any love interests?
Lord, no!
I'm having a dinner party tonight.
Have an extra seat. Why don't you swing by?
Sounds fun. What time?
Seven thirty.
You've got something up your sleeve?
Of course!
Tell me, Preston . . .
You'll see . . .
I hate and adore you at the same time.
What's a former Master for, if not that?
See you tonight!

I had always been completely in control of my life. Everything had always gone according to my plan. Even on my thirteenth birthday when I was sitting at dinner at Don Pablo's with my family, I was in control. When the mark appeared on the side of my face—a bright blue fire-shaped mark that ran from my left earlobe to almost the middle of my chin—I was still in control of how I dealt with it.

The shocked look on my family's faces did nothing to faze me. I had been expecting the mark to appear for about a month before my birthday. All fathers hold their breaths on their sons' thirteenth birthday, but I had already warned mine that I thought it might happen.

The mark signified that I was a man who was sexually attracted to other men. I lived in a world full of men—the females had long ago been separated from us and we had never seen them since. Our world was pretty simple—you were either marked or non-marked.

Non-marked men, or NOMARs, were the vast majority of our population. Some people estimated that they were ninety-five percent of the population, which made marked men very unusual. Your thirteenth birthday was the time when you were sorted into one group or the other.

Marked men had a difficult path to walk in our world, because NOMARs were constantly horny and marked men were easy targets. Centuries ago, a government agency called The Service was established to help with these and other issues facing these special men.

One thing The Service established were schools called Service Academies. These schools were only for marked men and let them learn in a safe environment with their peers. It was good for them both socially and for safety. NOMARs considered the SA to be sex academies, since many students received lessons in the erotic arts as well as the normal school subjects.

The Service was also responsible for the second major program that marked men could apply for, which was the one that usually changed their lives. When a marked man reached eighteen, he could enter into a contract with a wealthy NOMAR to become his sexual Servant for one to two years. The NOMAR paid one million dollars a year for this service and the marked man collected that fee at the end of their Service.

For many marked men, entering The Service and getting called for by a NOMAR was a life-changing experience. The money alone could change someone forever, but the chance to see the world, meet interesting and powerful people, and the chance at sexual satisfaction was too hard to resist in most cases.

Those reasons were not the impetus for me to enter The Service, however. I had gone to the SA and graduated at the top of my class. While my fellow classmates were falling in love with each other, I was not. I had a thing for non-marked men and I entered The Service to fall in love.

Love was a taboo topic for marked men, unless you were talking about with each other. It was a terrible faux-pas to fall in love with your Master or any other NOMAR. No one really knew why, maybe it was because the perception of spreading your legs because your Master told you to and not because you love to get fucked was more tolerable to the outside world.

I had studied hard while at The Service Academy and learned a lot. I wasn't just at the top of my class in academics, but I was one of the most sought after marked men to bang. I had learned how to please a NOMAR both in his bed and outside of it, and I looked forward every day to being called to Service by one of them.

That call came the week before my eighteenth birthday. I would be with my new Master by the end of the week. I was a giant ball of hopeful sexual energy and then I met Preston Sway the Third. Preston was a wealthy blue-blood who considered himself an art dealer, even though he rarely dealt it.

As far as Masters went, Preston was a nice man and treated me very fairly. Some of my marked friends had been placed with mean and cruel Masters who used them for their sexual pleasure, loaned them out to business contacts, or ignored them completely. I felt lucky to have been called by a Master who valued, included, and respected me.

However, there was no love between Preston and I. He was in his early sixties and more ballet dancer than lumberjack. He was not very masculine and really didn't do anything for me sexually at all. To Preston's credit, he didn't let our obvious non-attraction to each other affect our relationship. He was looking for me to be more friend and companion than sex object.

After coming to terms with the fact that I wasn't delivered to a Master that I would fall in love with, I came to terms with being Preston's companion and the fact that he was paying me for it made it even more palatable. Preston was a very good friend, made smart decisions, was a savvy business person, and had a tremendous network of people with which he had connected. He taught me everything he knew. By the time my third year with him was completed, I was three million dollars richer and networked with people in positions of power in almost every major field of commerce.

Preston and I had stayed in touch and had even vacationed together after my time in The Service. I counted myself lucky to have someone close to me like him. In the year after my time in The Service, I travelled and enjoyed time with friends, but above all, I fucked around. I made up for lost time by trying to find a NOMAR to be my Master, but so far had not found him.

Thanks to Preston's advice, I had invested my money wisely and was now living off the interest that my money was making without spending any of the capital. I was financially stable but not as happy as I should have been. There was something missing and I knew exactly what it was.

So, when an unusual opportunity came my way, I was so ready to accept it. After being in The Service, I stayed in the Washington, DC area where Preston lived rather than returning to the south where I was born because I had so many connections there. It was at one of Preston's dinner parties that I met Gray Carron.

I was aware of him the second Gray walked into the formal dining room where I was chatting with one of the White House aides that were attending the party. It's weird, but my nose started to itch and then I smelled him. I had always thought that everyone could smell pheromones like I could, but I found out pretty quickly that it was an unusual ability. I could usually smell a good-looking man immediately when he entered a room where I was located.

Gray was the tallest person in the room, which was saying something since I was over six feet three inches myself. More striking than his height was his size. Gray was a bruiser and all man—just the kind of NOMAR that I couldn't usually resist. He was blonde with a military crew cut and a square jaw that made me want to remove my clothes immediately.

The gathered crowd broke into applause when Gray appeared. I leaned over and asked my friend what was going on. "Who is that?"

Evan said, "That is Gray Carron."

"Why is everyone congratulating him?" I asked without taking my eyes off of the new arrival.

"He just got appointed by the President this afternoon."

"Appointed to what?"

"He's a new Ambassador, I think."

"Ambassador to where?"

"Eastern Europe somewhere," Evan said with a shrug of his shoulders as he grabbed another canape off of a big silver platter being carried near us.

Gray Carron's dark eyes locked onto mine almost immediately after he scanned the room to see who was in attendance. I managed a small smile and forced myself to look away.

My former Master swept into the room and announced that dinner was ready. As at all of Preston's dinner parties, the guests had to stand until he announced everyone's seating assignment. Preston loved to mix up the order of who sat with whom and his decisions seemed to be based on the latest, most up-to-date happenings in the capital.

Preston went around the table and finally called my name at the opposite side of his. I stood behind my chair. I was next to Preston's best friend, Robert, who was at the foot of the table. I liked Robert and would enjoy catching up with him.

Preston was taking great delight in the suspense and drama of his seating assignments, so I smiled at the ridiculous look of glee on his visage.

"Next I think will be, Gray. Yes, Mr. Carron, if you please." Preston turned to me and whispered, "You're welcome."

I felt the familiar tingling in my balls that usually signaled that I was going to get a hard-on as I watched the graceful but powerful body of Gray Carron come towards me. We shook hands and the warmth of his skin did nothing to reduce my hard cock.

"You are Sutton, are you not?" he asked me as we sat down.

"I am. And you are Gray Carron?"

"Yes," he answered as we put our napkins into our laps.

I hoped he was not looking at my lap, but I was sure looking at his. I said hello to Robert before I turned back to Gray. "Congratulations on your appointment."

"Thank you. It's been a real whirlwind of a day." He

turned to me and seemed to really study me.

"I didn't hear in which country you will be living."

"Romania," he said easily.

"Oh, really?"

"You have been there?" he asked as we were served our soup course.

"No, but I'm kinda obsessed with it," I admitted, feeling myself flush slightly.

"Really?"

"I'm a huge Dracula fan," I explained.

Gray's dark eyes twinkled with delight. "Ah, then you must come visit and see the castle."

"I would like that," I said, a little too quickly. I took a beat and breathed in deeply. Gray Carron smelled like firewood and McIntosh apples. Smells were very important to me and I liked both of those. "So, you have been there already?"

"Oh, yes. My family is from Romania, originally. One of my brothers still lives there."

"Oh, cool," I said foolishly, not knowing what to say to that.

"I leave for Bucharest tomorrow."

"Wow, so fast," I commented.

"I wanted to get started right away."

I nodded as I swallowed some of the cream of asparagus soup.

"And I hear that your Service to Preston has ended."

"It has."

"And what will you do now with your new-found wealth?"

"New-found?" I snorted. "I worked hard for that money."

When Gray spoke next, his voice was twice as husky as it had been. "You didn't work as hard under Preston as you would have under me."

I looked at him, unable to look away. His words were

making my blood boil with lust and need as I visualized the scene in my head. "Oh, yeah?" I finally was able to croak.

"Oh, yeah," he said firmly. "You will come to my hotel room tonight and I will show you how a Master should have treated you, Sutton Pike." His voice smoldered with sexual tension. He turned towards me, grabbed his wine glass and asked, "What do you say to that?"

"Okay," I agreed, completely caught off-guard by this beautiful man and his exciting words.

He narrowed his eyes and shook his head slightly left and right.

"Yes, Sir?" I whispered.

Gray Carron smiled a beautiful grin and clinked his crystal glass against mine. "Now, you're talking."

CHAPTER TWO

A text string between Sutton Pike and his best friends later that same night:

Met someone tonight . . .
Who?
A politician . . .
POTUS?
Hardly. The new ambassador to Romania . . .
Sounds stuffy . . .
He's going to be stuffing me shortly . . .
No way! Hot?
Uber-hot! Unfortunately he leaves for Europe tomorrow.
On the way to his hotel now . . .
You know our rule – when you go home with a NOMAR,
you tell us the information and we make sure you
get home safely. What's his name?
Gray Carron . . . google that mug
Hotel?
Carlysle Dupont Circle
Stay safe but be bad!
You know I will.

I had just finished texting Adam and Justin. We had made a pact at school to always let each other know when we were going home with a NOMAR. There were no exceptions, even if he was a United States Ambassador. It turned out that I was a much bigger whore than they were, but I felt safer having them know the information in case something happened to me.

The Service had been able to pass laws protecting marked men, but that didn't stop lust-crazed psychopaths from kidnapping and raping us. Most of the men that I associated with were law-abiding and respectful, but you could never tell about a person until you were alone with them.

I was in the back of a sleek Town Car with Gray Carron. He had a big hand gripped around the inside of my thigh, closer to my knee than my nuts, but pleasantly intimate none-the-less. The amount of body heat that was being transferred between Gray's hand and my leg was tremendous.

We had not said a word to each other after dinner was finished. We had stayed for a drink but then said our good-byes. Preston grinned like a possum when he saw that we were leaving together. The government car pulled up to the Carlysle Hotel and stopped in front of the door.

"Ten tomorrow to go to the airport," Gray told the driver.

"Yes, sir."

We both stepped out of the car and I let him lead the way to his room. The hotel was a great old art deco building that was still furnished in the style—all gleaming metal and mirrors. The elevator doors opened as soon as Gray touched the button.

As soon as the doors closed, Gray looked over at me and said, "My last night in the United States and my first night in you."

"First and last," I smirked.

"Maybe," he said mysteriously.

I was left to ponder that while I watched the doors open and we stepped right across the hall to one of the penthouse doors. Gray opened it with a key card and flipped the lights on. The room was immense and beautifully done, reminding me of the Empire State Building.

"Nothing but the best for the new Ambassador," I mumbled as I looked around.

"Correction, nothing but the best for the Carrons. The government barely pays for anything," he said with a laugh.

"You've always been wealthy?" I pried.

"Yes. You?"

"Just recently," I said with a grin.

"Thanks to Preston, of course."

"Of course."

Gray headed to the bar and asked, "Would you like a drink?"

"No, thanks," I told him. "I'll drink from the hose in a little bit."

I watched in delight as he had to swallow hard, his big Adam's apple making a marked decent and rise in his thick neck. He poured himself a Scotch in a heavy rocks glass and added a lot of ice from a bucket in the freezer.

"What are your plans with your new-found wealth and all your free time?" he asked as he took a seat in a comfortable-looking armchair facing me.

"I really don't have any plans," I admitted. "I wanted to travel some and I have done that. I wanted to connect with my friends again and I have also done that."

"A free spirit who likes to travel, huh?"

"A free spirit who likes to travel, but loves to fuck."

"Ah, so you are looking for a powerful man who also likes to fuck?"

"He doesn't have to be powerful . . ." I answered him by letting my statement end abruptly and just hang out there.

"No? I thought you were shopping around for a politician."

"No. DC is just where I was called to, so it is familiar. I

don't mind politicians, especially if they look like you." I straddled his legs and took a seat on his lap facing him.

"You may not like me," he said, seemingly completely immune to my charms.

"Why is that?"

"Because, unlike these other men that you have met, I know how to Master a Servant."

"Had a Servant before, have we?" I asked tracing the wetness of the Scotch on his lips with the tip of my finger.

"Yes."

"Show me," I said in a challenging tone.

"Stand," he ordered. The voice he used had changed. Gray had flipped into what I called Master-mode and I was impressed. I stood up.

"Good boy. Stand in front of me."

I moved back into the clearing right in front of him. He crossed his legs and took another sip of Scotch.

I started to unbutton my shirt and he growled at me, "Wait for my direction, young one."

Maybe he does know what he's doing . . .

Suddenly, I became aware of the tingle in my balls that alerted me to the fact that I was going to have a hard-on any minute. Gray was affecting me more than any man had in a long time.

I stood still waiting for his direction. He didn't seem to be in a rush, instead he took in every aspect of my body while slowly sipping his drink. I had never met a NOMAR with this much self-control before.

"Take your shoes and socks off, Sutton," he commanded me finally.

I kicked off my Bucks and leaned against the mantle behind me to take my socks off. Afterwards, I stood up straight and waited.

"And now the shirt."

I unbuttoned the top buttons, pulled it off over my head,

and threw it onto the couch beside me. I wondered if Gray liked my body or not. It was hard to tell with NOMARs because they usually just wanted you for your mouth and your ass, so they didn't pay much attention to anything else. Most of my friends at the Service Academy had been slight, thin, and short. I was not.

I was built like a linebacker on a football team—tall, thick, and muscular. I usually had more in common body-wise with the NOMARs than I did with the marked men. Not being able to tell from Gray's face, I hoped for the best.

"Turn around and face away from me, Sutton."

I did.

"Take your pants off. Slowly . . ."

I had done this little dance before. I unbuttoned my pants and unhooked my belt. Slowly, I shimmed out of my pants, making sure that I bent forward when I did to give the new ambassador a great view of my ass.

"A jock strap?" he asked. "I'm surprised."

"I got used to . . ."

"Silence!" he snapped, interrupting me just as his flat hand smacked me on the ass cheeks. "Don't speak unless I give you permission."

Wow! Where has this man been my entire life? I love the command he has over me.

I decided to test him. "Yes, sir."

"I do like the sound of that," he immediately said.

Well, he isn't perfect but he is pretty damn handsome.

"Come over here. I have something to keep your mouth busy, Sutton," he said in a voice laced with husky need.

I walked slowly in front of him again as he uncrossed his legs and spread them apart. I pushed the limits of his direction again by kneeling without permission. He was too busy pulling his cock out of his fly to correct me. I had my answer—Gray Carron was not the perfect man for me, but he seemed closer to him than anyone I had ever met before.

Taking his cock from him, I lowered my head to his crotch and inhaled the fragrant muskiness of it. His apple and firewood smell was intoxicating to me. Gray's cock was nice and thick, although an average length. I used my tongue to tease the soft skin of his cock head before wrapping my lips around it and sucking it into my mouth. I noticed the heat pouring off his skin—its intensity even higher than mine.

The ambassador tasted like clean masculinity and I quickly sucked his whole root into my hungry hole. Taking long drawing pulls on his dick, I sucked him for all he's worth. Gray moaned as I took his member out of my mouth and licked up and down the sides. Mr. Ambassador had removed his tie and had draped it around the back of my neck.

Gray was as hard as a length of pipe, so I looked up to see if he was ready to fuck. To my delight, his response was to grasp the sides of my shaven head and force my head further down onto his joint. He pumped his hips and soon exploded into my mouth. Strands of hot, salty man-juice hit the back of my throat and my tonsils. I swallowed Gray's seed down and milked him for more. He continued to force my head down onto his meat by pulling on both sides of the tie that he had wrapped around my neck.

"Hot little mouth," Gray said when he finally stopped convulsing and was able to speak again.

I sat back on my haunches and waited on his next command. It was my next test for him. Could he go again immediately or would he need to rest some first?

Gray Carron took a big sip of his scotch and smiled at me.

I wondered what he was thinking. I was thinking that I was ready to be underneath this stud as he pounded my pud repeatedly. He stood up and went to pour himself another drink.

Turning around, he walked into the bedroom portion of the suite and out of my view. I could hear a sound every once in a while but not enough to be able to figure out what he was doing. I was getting tired of kneeling but I was thrilled that this man had the willpower and the confidence to be so in control of me.

Gray appeared again and poured another drink. He walked over to me and held the glass to my lips. "Drink," he commanded.

My mouth was dry and still had the strong taste of his cum, so I opened my mouth and let the amber liquid enter me. It burned like fire, but a good cleansing fire that continued down my throat and into my belly.

"You might just make a good little pet, after all, Sutton Pike."

You don't know how headstrong I can be, Gray . . .

"Shall we begin?" he asked with a raised eyebrow.

"Yes, sir," I replied as I watched him uncoil his tie from his hand. *What the fuck is he going to do with that?*

CHAPTER THREE

Part of a text string between Justin and Adam, Sutton's best friends, later that same night:

Do you think Sutton seems off a little?
Yes, I noticed.
What do you think it is?
I don't know, but my guess is that he wants to find someone.
Someone to be with all the time, like you have Brice and I have Thad?
I think so. He seems lonely to me.
Me too.
I tried to set him up with some guys, but they weren't right.
It's harder with him because he's drawn to NOMARs.
I know. I'm not sure NOMARs are capable of what he wants . . .
Maybe this ambassador could be the one . . .
Maybe.
And there are so many NOMARs to choose from . . .
That's part of the problem, I think.
It could be worse. He's got money and having a lot of sex.
Sounds fun, doesn't it?
LOL!

Gray Carron was a little bit of a freak.

I was currently kneeling in front of his hotel bed and I had a good sight of several things that he had laid out on the bed. The newest US ambassador to Romania had attached

16

his tie around my neck and led me like a dog on all fours into the bedroom.

I didn't mind debasing myself a little if the fuck was worth it, so I was hoping that this one was going to be. Once in the bedroom, Gray had told me to kneel at the base of the bed. His tie was still around my thick throat.

On the bed were two more ties, as well as a tube of lube, two bottles of water, a hotel hand towel, a leather dog collar, and a leather harness. I wasn't surprised that the budding politician had such a dark little secret but really shocked that he travelled with the tools of his fetish.

Gray was in the bathroom and when he came back into the bedroom, he was completely nude except for leather wristbands, strips of black leather on the tops of his biceps, and a leather thong wrapped around the top of his nut sack, which caused it to stand up and out from his body.

Gray Carron was probably in his early forties, almost twenty years my senior, but he had a body that any man would trade for at any age. His tall frame held an athlete's body with muscular pecs, six-pack abs, walnut-cracking thighs, and bulging biceps. His ass was sublime when he turned to the side and I loved that his cock was stiff again. He didn't quite have the bulk that I usually liked in a lover, but he would definitely do.

"Let's get you dressed so that we can get started, Sutton," Gray said with obvious delight in his voice. He walked towards me with his stiff cock swaying in front of him and removed the tie from my throat. He replaced it with the leather dog collar and then ran the tie through one of the metal loops on it.

Gray seemed to enjoy dragging the silk fabric across my body and face as he hooked the tie onto my collar. "Arms in the air, Sutton," he commanded.

I lifted my arms into the air and he slid the harness down

over my arms, head, and shoulders. Having used a harness several times before, I knew their main purpose was to allow the fucker to get a grip on the one being fucked and to manipulate his body to better the pleasure.

Gray leaned down and buckled the harness around my chest. His neck was exposed and oh so close to my lips. I inhaled deeply and was just about to lick his neck when he stopped me cold.

"Don't even think about it," he growled.

I drew back, appreciating his control.

"Hands behind your back, Sutton."

I smiled ever so slightly as I put my hands in the small of my back and grasped them together. Gray walked around behind me and tied my hands securely with one of the ties from the bed. He knew his knots and soon had my hands tied as expertly as a cowboy binds a calf at the rodeo.

Gray leaned down and whispered into my ear, "You are a beautiful little pet, Sutton."

And you are a very handsome and sexy Master, Gray . . .

"Stand," he ordered as he pulled up on the tie connected to my collar.

I stood up and he walked around me, his dick so hard that it pointed to the heavens.

"I'm afraid that I can't wait any longer, my pet. Kneel on the bed, Sutton."

I climbed up onto the bed and knelt in the middle. Gray spread my knees with his own as he climbed up with me. He placed his palm in the middle of my back and pushed it forward. My head hit the mattress and I turned my face to the side so it was more comfortable.

Gray used the lube to slicken the hard sausage against his belly and then fed it into my hole. I enjoyed the feeling of him punching a hole inside me and I definitely loved when my puckered hole stretched itself around his hard shaft and then squeezed it tightly. This unbelievable warmth radiated out from his prick, heating my insides.

"Oh, fuck! Where did my little pet get such a tight hole?" he asked, his voice completely transformed by husky lust.

"It's just for you, sir," I said, playing my part to get him worked up even more.

"Weren't you in The Service, Sutton?"

"Yes, sir."

"Preston must not have ever fucked you, huh?"

"My ass has always been able to bounce back, sir."

"Well, I am very pleased with it so far. We shall see how it bounces back from this because I plan on being planted inside you for at least the next five or six hours."

Five or six hours? Why couldn't I have met this man a year ago?

Gray began to fuck and he was seriously good at it. He built to a fast pace and used the harness to move me back and forth over his hot shaft when he got tired of pounding me himself. Sometimes, he would pull on my arms that were tied behind my back like they were the reins of the horse he had at a fast gallop.

When I felt that my new, commanding friend was close to his climax, I focused extra hard on squeezing his prick with my ass muscles as he tried to pull out during each stroke. Gray responded by pulling on the tie hooked to my collar until I was straight up and down. He held me there, looping the silk tie around his hand as he hunched over my up-turned ass and fucked me harder than shit.

After the ambassador bred my ass and had pumped his cock into me until he was too limp to continue, he lay flat on my back breathing heavily. We were both sweating like pigs. I loved his heavy form on top of me—pressing me down into the mattress and mingling our sweaty bodies together as one.

"That was fucking awesome," he finally said into the back of my head.

"Yeah, it was!" I said, laughing.

True to his word, Gray only took a quick break before railing me out again, this time lying on my back while my hands were tied to the bedposts. The new ambassador tied my knees to the bottom of the harness and then gave me a real hard fuck.

After Gray dumped another load of hot cum in my ass, he lay down beside me breathing deeply. "Well, that was unexpected."

"Not what you wanted?" I prompted him for a compliment.

"No, better than I imagined."

"I aim to please . . ."

"You certainly do."

There was a silence that hung between us. It was easy and nice, even though I was still tied in a compromising position.

"My father got a Servant once when I was a teenager," Gray said as he rolled onto his side to face me. "I mean, he always had a Servant. I practiced fucking on my father and grandfather's Servants growing up, but this one was special."

"Special?"

"My father had requested a Servant who had not gone to the SA. Now that I think about it, he probably requested a virgin, if that was possible."

I chuckled and wondered if there was such a thing.

"He came to us when I was fifteen. His name was Shane and he was eighteen. One of the least attractive guys I have ever seen and clumsy as hell in bed, but he did seem to be innocent in almost every way." Gray had a far-away look in his eyes like he was visualizing a memory.

"I bet he was scared of you and your family."

"He probably was. Shane had the tightest asshole I had ever fucked, and I couldn't get enough of it. I probably spent more time with that Servant than I did with all the rest combined."

"I'm surprised your father allowed that."

"He got real mad at me when he found out how often I had been nailing him."

I laughed. "I bet."

Gray suddenly looked me in the eyes, and I could see that he was in the here-and-now. "Your ass reminds me of Shane's."

This really made me laugh. "I'm no virgin, Gray."

"I know, but you've got a sweet asshole."

"Thanks! Your cock is not so bad either." I saw that the very thing that I had mentioned was starting to bloat with blood again. "Your stamina is unbelievable."

"Your ass is the closest thing I have ever found to Shane's."

"And?" I prompted him.

"And I'm going to need to give it another try just to make sure."

"If you have to, sir . . ."

"Oh, I have to, my pet." Gray unhooked the ties from the bed and rolled me on top of him. I straddled his body and let him feed his cock back into my puckered hole.

"Fuck!" he groaned from below me. "How are you doing that?"

"It's magic," I said flippantly as I held onto his legs and bounced my ass up and down on top of his crotch. There was nothing in the world better than the feeling of my asshole being stretched around a hard cock and then being worked up and down that thing. Or, if there was, I had never found it. Of course, the thicker the cock, the more pleasure in my book.

Gray was doing just fine. He took back control by pulling me towards him until I was lying on top of his broad chest.

"Put your feet on top of my thighs, pet."

I did, feeling his hands grab my upper thighs. He spread them and held me secure as he fucked me hard and fast from below.

Gray fucked just the way I liked—hard and fast. He commanded me almost the way I needed to be controlled. He was handsome and interesting with a great job. He had a good cock and fantastic sexual stamina. I knew in my heart that he didn't quite live up to my ideal man, but suddenly I wondered if that could be enough for me.

CHAPTER FOUR

Excerpt from an online notebook kept by Sutton Pike:

April twenty-first: Gray; Washington DC
US Ambassador to Romania & Dom, 42
Fucked for over four hours
Face: Ghost Pepper
Body: Ghost Pepper
Dick: Jalapeno

April twentieth: Luis; Airport
Airport security guard, 24
Blew him and fucked in a detention cell
Face: Banana Pepper
Body: Ghost Pepper
Dick: Habanero

April nineteenth: Ragheb; Seychelles
Indian businessman, 55
Spent my last night of vacation in his bed
Face: Poblano
Body: Jalapeno
Dick: Habanero

Gray Carron was still sleeping soundly beside me when I put my phone back onto the wireless charging station on the nightstand. I had just updated my sex file and was now considering getting some sleep.

I was usually a night owl. I could usually go all night and then sleep during the day. It had kept me safe many times after fucking around with a NOMAR. They would usually fall to sleep, leaving me the opportunity to get the hell out of the situation if I wasn't happy or to snoop through their stuff to see what kind of man they really were if I was happy.

Gray had almost lived up to his promise. He had fucked me for over four hours before he collapsed. It was impressive and I was still looking at him in awe. He had told me that I could spend the rest of the day in this hotel room if I wanted to, so that was my plan.

I lay down beside Gray and ran my hand softly over his spiky haircut. This man might just be someone that I could get used to. I closed my eyes and fell right to sleep breathing in deeply of his scent while being warmed by his hot body.

Gray woke me up a couple of hours later. When I drowsily opened my eyes again, he was showered and dressed in an expensive dark suit and his bags were packed.

"Hi, sleepy head," Gray said softly as he pushed a stray strand of my hair from my forehead back in place.

"Hey," I said back in a husky sleep-filled voice.

Gray sat down on the edge of the bed.

"You look great," I complimented him.

"Thanks, pet. Listen, I wanted to talk to you quickly before I go."

"Okay," I said sitting more upright in the bed, my back against the headboard and pillows.

"I really had fun with you last night."

"Thanks. Me too."

"You've got a sweet ass that I can't seem to get enough of . . ."

"Lucky me," I smirked.

"When I suggested that you come visit me in Romania, I

was serious, Sutton."

"And I am seriously considering it, Gray," I told him.

He looked at me strangely for a second, tilting his head. "I thought you were just humoring me."

I laughed softly. "It's a country that I've dreamed of visiting, and there is a man there that can fuck for four hours, so why wouldn't I seriously consider it?"

He chuckled and asked, "So, you would seriously come?"

"Of course."

He took a deep breath. "Would you consider being my pet?"

"Your pet?"

"I think I could make you happy, Sutton," he admitted with a rush of words.

"You mean live there with you?"

"Yes," he answered and then held his breath.

I was shocked. Would I be happy living with him? Maybe I could try it and then change my mind.

"I could find you a job there if you want to work."

"Gray," I answered with a smile, "I need to think about it for a little while, but I am thrilled that you asked."

"So, you will consider it?" He looked so hopeful that I couldn't help but beam at him.

"Yes. Can I let you know by the end of the month?"

"Absolutely. I will wait to hear from you." Gray stood up and then reached over and stroked my face. "I'm glad I met you, Sutton."

"Same. Have a great trip and good luck, Gray."

"Thanks." He grabbed the handle of his suitcase and wheeled it out of the room after him.

The hotel door slammed shut and the enveloping silence pressed in on me like a weight. Gray had stunned me by asking me to come and live with him. I barely knew him, but what I did know, I liked.

I lay back down and smiled to myself as I closed my eyes. I was soon asleep again dreaming of living in Dracula's castle with Gray in Romania.

I woke in the late afternoon and took a quick shower in the fancy hotel bathroom. My ass was sore from my night of fucking, but I was happy as a clam that I finally had some kind of focus to my life. Having an option made all the difference in the world.

I got dressed in my clothes from last night and did the walk of shame back to my apartment, stopping at a local deli to get a chicken salad sandwich and a bag of chips to take with me. I sat in front of the TV and ate, choosing a baseball game to watch because I couldn't concentrate on anything except the talk that Gray and I had finished this morning.

Preston called me later that night and I filled him in on the news. He was shocked that I was considering the move but was supportive of any decision that I chose. He assured me that Gray Carron was a good man from what he knew of him and his family. I told him that I was definitely going to have to think about it before I could make a decision one way or the other.

I stayed at home that night, alone with my thoughts. But by the next night, I was more than ready to go out again. I called a friend of mine named Gordy who agreed to go out with me. Gordy was a NOMAR, but we had decided to be friends many years ago. I liked going out with Gordy because most NOMARs assumed he was my Master and left me alone, which left me with the chance to troll for who I wanted to take home. Gordy had come to terms with the fact that I would always be leaving with someone else a long time ago.

Dressing in a tight t-shirt and my best jeans, I poured myself a drink and waited on Gordy to text me that he was outside. I looked at my phone and saw that I had a text. It was from Gray.

Hey. Hope you made it home safely . . .
I did, thanks! Are you already in Romania?
Yes. The weather is good. Wanna try it out?
LOL. I'm def going to come . . .
You will come alright . . .
Hmmm!
Vacation or pet?
Undecided as of yet . . .
But still considering it?
Yes
I miss your ass already . . .
There are a lot of things I miss about you . . .
Ah, so I have a chance . . .
Haha! A better one than you know.
Good. Well, goodnight, Sutton.
Night, Gray.

Gordy's text that he was here came just as I was finishing with Gray. I left the apartment, locked the door behind me, and joined him on the front sidewalk.

"Hey," Gordy said when he looked up from his phone.

"Uber?" I asked.

"Sure. So, what's been happening?" he asked as I called for the nearest car.

"I met a guy the other night at one of Preston's dinner parties," I said off-handedly.

"No way," he said in shock.

"Way."

"Who was he? One of those stuffy politicians that Preston likes so much?"

"Yeah, but I wound up being stuffed."

"You like him?"

"He was pretty damn sexy." The Uber pulled up and we

piled inside.

"You seeing him again?" Gordy asked.

"I would, but he left for Romania yesterday."

Gordy couldn't have looked more shocked. "Romania?"

I smirked, "Yeah. He's the ambassador."

"Seriously?"

"Seriously."

"So, that happened. What's next?" Gordy asked.

We chatted about possibly visiting Romania until the Uber driver pulled over in front of a huge nightclub in the warehouse district.

Gordy liked to drink and watch sports and I liked to drink and watch men, so this was the perfect hangout for us — half sports bar and half Service Station. A Service Station was a place where NOMARs could go to have sex in our world. Usually they were stand-alone buildings where men could go, pay for a certain time, and have a variety of holes to shove their dicks into.

This nightclub, called the Slam and Dunk, was a huge open room with leather couches and recliners facing gigantic TV screens on the walls. Right in the middle of the madness were multiple bars. Waiters were constantly hustling between the seating areas, serving some of the city's best food as well as the libations.

As soon as the doors opened, I took a big whiff of the cavernous room. My nose told me that there were several men in this big room who were going to compete to fuck me tonight.

I grinned like a fool at my friend as I took his arm and headed into the nightclub. "In answer to your question, Gordy, I'm not sure what's next, but I'm positive he's in here."

CHAPTER FIVE

A phone conversation between Sutton Pike and his father, Robert, held in the hallway of the club that night:

Hi, Dad.
Sutton, my boy. You watching the game?
I am. Good, isn't it?
They are doing okay. You doing okay?
Yes, sir.
You sure? What have you been up to?
You know, a little of this and a little of that.
If I know you, it's a lot of . . . that.
Dad!
I know. We're not supposed to talk about that, but I worry about your safety.
I'm being safe, Dad.
Good. Make sure you do.
Always. Listen, Dad, I might be moving soon.
Oh, yeah? Where to?
Romania maybe. I'm not sure yet.
That's a long way away. I would worry about you . . .

My father would worry about me if I moved to Romania and got my brains fucked out every day, but what would he say if he knew that I was doing the same thing here in America, every day with different strangers? He would probably be more worried.

"What do you smell?" Gordy asked me when I was finished talking to my father on my cell phone and had returned to the couch where we were watching Mike Trout destroy the Diamondbacks.

"I smell several men," I explained. Gordy was used to my way of hooking up with NOMARs by now and seemed to be fascinated with the process. I was always willing to oblige him.

"Who?" He looked around curiously.

"There is one over near the far TV," I said, pointing, "and a huge smell over by the middle bar."

"How do you do that?" he asked in wonder.

"It's a gift," I said as I raised my hands and shoulders.

"Which shall it be?" Gordy goaded me.

"I don't know, but I have to at least see why the one at the bar smells so strongly."

The NOMAR from the far TV set made his way towards me first. He was probably in his late twenties and wearing a soccer jersey. His black hair came to a point on his forehead and there was a tattooed band around his wrist. I noticed his expressive eyes immediately.

He seemed shocked to see me when he walked in front of our couch. But due to his cocky nature and unbelievable confidence, he was able to recover and turn around. He stopped right in front of me.

"I'm Rocko," he said.

"Of course, you are," I smirked.

"You with him?" he asked, nodding at Gordy.

"He's my friend and I'm here with him," I enlightened him.

"You coming home with me?" Rocko asked with a grin.

"Not much for words, huh, Rocko?"

"Nope."

I considered him for a couple of seconds. He was the

stereotypical Jersey or New York Italian boy — in his twenties, brash as hell, dark hair swept back, too tan, too muscled, tats on his forearms, and teeth as big and white as Chicklets. I didn't normally like his kind and he was no different.

I enjoyed confidence just as much as the next marked man, but I needed a little subtlety or humility with mine as well. I was still considering him when he pressed me for an answer. In the back of my head, I knew that I was still intrigued by whoever was producing the uber-smell over by the bar. I had to investigate that or I would always wonder.

I said, firmly, "I got plans already tonight, Rocko."

"Tomorrow?" he immediately asked.

"I'm going into The Service tomorrow," I immediately answered. His look of surprise was exactly how all NOMARs reacted when I used this lie. I had found it to be most effective throughout the years when I wanted to shut down one of them.

"The Service?"

"Yep. I'll be completely naked and locked in a cage tomorrow, headed towards my Master." I knew the visual was one that he was already experiencing in his head, so there was no harm in confirming it for him.

Rocko smiled broadly. "Even more of a reason why you need this tonight, then."

"Of course," I agreed with him. "You're timing is just off, man. If I wouldn't have already committed to another party . . ."

Rocko suddenly looked very deflated.

"Maybe in two years, when I return from Service," I said to make him feel better.

"Yeah," he said, dejectedly. He turned to continue on his way out of the club.

I watched him go, making sure that he left.

Gordy leaned over. "Was that one of them?"

"Yes. The weaker of the two smells."

"What was it?"

I chuckled. "You are going to laugh."

"You have to tell me now."

I rolled my eyes. "Philly cheesesteak and fresh cut grass."

"What the fuck?" Gordy asked, already laughing hard.

"You wanted to know, Gordy. I'm going to go to the bathroom and then I'm going to try to locate Mr. Smelly at the bar. Keep an eye on me, will you?"

"Sure thing. Want me to come with you?"

"No, I got it."

I walked quickly to the bathroom looking at all the men in the room and quickly evaluating each one of them. I didn't make eye contact or linger on any one guy because I didn't need to send the wrong message.

Bathrooms were dangerous places for marked men due to the small quarters and the state of undress, so I quickly pissed and washed my hands. I had to deal with one drunk guy trying to paw me afterwards, but I easily sidestepped his sluggish advances.

I made my way out to the center bar and tried to locate my man. It wasn't hard, even though I was getting interference from forty or so men standing and sitting around the area. I took a seat that was open and awkwardly pulled myself up to the bar.

The NOMARs around me didn't quite know what to say, so most of them just openly stared, slack-jawed. Opening my nasal cavity, I located the smell and it was right in front of me.

Is it the bartender?

I tracked him with my eyes. He smelled like lime zest and the raw leather that I'd worked with as a child in Boy Scouts. He was one of four bartenders inside the huge horseshoe-shaped bar. His back was constantly to me, but I knew if I stared at it long enough, he would turn around. He was wearing black military boots, jeans, and a very tight black t-shirt. His dark hair was shiny and pulled back into a man bun.

The bartender did finally turn around. In his early thirties, I assumed, and built like a soldier. He smiled at me when he saw me and came right over. He had a dark tan and his biceps were so big that they wouldn't fit inside his black t-shirt sleeves. His big, square chin had a day's worth of heavy growth on it.

"Nice mark, man," he said as he wiped the bar in front of me.

"Thanks." I noticed that his smell wasn't quite right. It was the correct smell, just not strong enough. I was terribly confused by this man.

"I'm Milo. What can I get for you?"

"Sutton. I'll take a Long Island Iced Tea." I knew that it would take him a minute to make it and it would buy me time to figure out what was wrong with my nose.

Milo had started to make my drink when he was suddenly joined by one of the other bartenders. I knew from the smell right away that they were twins. They looked alike, had the same bodies, and the same jet-black hair. Their combined scents meshed into the correct strength and odor.

But there were also enough differences to tell them apart. The new twin had a full black beard, short hair shaved on the sides, and both arms and hands tatted.

"What's your brother's name, Milo?" I asked loudly.

"This is Arlo," Milo introduced me.

Arlo had the same beautiful smile as his twin. "Sutton," I said, shaking hands. "You boys new here?" I asked, already knowing the answer.

"Just started last week." Milo handed me my drink.

"Welcome." I toasted them with my upheld glass.

"When do we get to start with you?" Arlo asked with a grin.

Taking a sip of the sweet cocktail first, I put my glass down and answered, "I don't know about starting since you guys are working right now, but you definitely can finish with me."

"Oh, yeah?" Milo asked flirtatiously. "We both get off in two hours."

"I hope to be getting off shortly thereafter," I said with a laugh. The boys laughed easily at my crude humor. "You guys ever fucked together before?" I was suddenly aware that the men around me had become very interested in our conversation. I was taking a risk by talking about sex in such a public place with NOMARs who were drinking and listening in, but I found it very difficult to resist.

"You mean, besides at a Service Station?"

"Yeah."

The twins were leaning on the bar towards me. Milo looked at his brother and said, "There was that time in high school."

"Ah, do tell," I egged them on.

Arlo picked up the story. "We were both on the soccer team in high school. We were seniors and one of the freshmen players was a marked guy who had been letting us fuck him for most of the season."

"Together?" I asked.

"No, separately," Milo answered. "We won the championship that year and the marked guy, David, was so excited that he told the team that he was going to be their cum dump after the game."

Arlo added, "It was the first time that we had fucked somebody together."

"Did you spit roast him?" I asked.

"No, but you can show us how," Arlo said with a smirk.

"My pleasure," I told them.

"I'm pretty sure it will be our pleasure," Milo retorted.

"Until then." I took my drink and left behind a fifty-dollar bill. I knew the brothers were watching my ass as I walked away, and I enjoyed their eyes on me.

CHAPTER SIX

A text string between Sutton Pike and his best friends later that same night:

Going home with the bartenders tonight, fellas
Bartenders?
Yeah, I know . . . kinda pathetic.
But you should see them . . .
Hot?
Twins
No way!
Yes way!!!
Hot twins? You are such a slut!
I know!
I also know both of you former-sluts are jealous as hell!
That we are!
Your place or theirs?
Please! They are bartenders . . . we're going to my place.
Names?
Milo and Arlo
Stay safe
Gordy will drop us off at the apartment.

Gordy and I finished watching the game with the occasional interference from drunks who wanted to harass me. I was pretty skilled at protecting myself and Gordy helped a lot. We only had to wait a little longer for the twins to get off work.

"You sure you want to do this?" Gordy asked as we waited.

"Oh, yeah," I smirked.

"Are they going to be respectful?"

"They better be."

"You know what to do if they aren't," Gordy quizzed me.

"Yes, Dad," I said sarcastically.

"Just trying to keep you safe," he said with his hands turned up in supplication.

"And I appreciate it, Gordo," I said with a grin. "You've been a very good friend to me."

"I like hanging out with you. Makes me feel important and powerful."

"Like a Master?" I asked him.

"Yeah, I guess so," he admitted.

Gordy had a great job working with the Secretary of State. I figured that with his connections, that he would be famous and successful for the rest of his career. "Is that something that you would like to be?"

He chuckled. "What NOMAR doesn't want that?"

"Well, yeah," I admitted.

"I won't be able to afford it for quite a while, but then I very much would want to give it a go."

"You would probably make a very good Master, Gordy."

He smiled shyly. "Why do you say that?"

"You are always thinking about my safety and that is su-per-important for a Master." He nodded, so I continued, "You are fun to be around, easy to talk to, attentive, and compassionate."

"Thanks for saying those things, Sutton." He blushed slightly.

"No problem, Gordy. You're a catch. Any Servant would be happy to crawl out of their cage for you."

"Do you think he would be happy with me sexually?" he shyly asked me, finally.

"Nothing turns on a Servant like a Master who is confident and knows how to command, Gordy. If you can do that, he will eat out of your hand . . . and anywhere else you tell him to."

Gordy smiled and patted me on the back. "I think your twin trouble is coming this way."

I turned and waved at the two muscle heads meandering between the couches, tables, and people towards us. I introduced Arlo and Milo to Gordy and then we headed out of the club. The boys had a car, so we rode with them back to my place.

"You sure you are okay?" Gordy asked me one final time before he left.

"I'm sure. I'll call you tomorrow, Gordy."

"You do that." He stepped into the Uber cab I had called for him.

I waved to him and then turned to the twins. "You boys ready to go?"

They both smiled broadly and said, "Hell, fucking, yes!"

"Let's do it." I led the way into the vestibule, used my key card to gain entrance, said hello to the security guard in the lobby, and used my key to get the elevator doors to open.

"Tight security," Milo remarked.

"I don't want anything happening to me . . . that I don't ask for," I smirked to him.

"It is good of you to be careful, especially if you are bringing NOMARs back here with you," Arlo said.

I stepped towards them in the elevator and reached out a hand to each of their crotches. I grabbed the outlines of their cocks through their jeans and said, "What kind of marked man do you think I am?"

Arlo spluttered and said, "I didn't mean—"

I interrupted him. "I'm just jagging you, you big lug. I'm exactly that kind of marked man . . ."

The doors opened and I led them to my apartment and let them inside.

"Want a drink?" I asked.

"Beer," they both said.

I grabbed two bottles for each man from the kitchen and handed them over while I poured myself a glass of rum over ice. Leading them back to my bedroom, I heard the gasps behind me as the twins got their first look at my oversized bed and the leather sling hanging from my ceiling.

"Which one do you want to play on first?" I asked with a sly smile as I took a sip of the cold alcohol in my glass.

The twins looked at each other with confused looks for just a second and then quickly started to strip off their clothes. I laughed as I put my drink down on the nightstand and followed suit. We were soon naked and I was on my knees on the thick carpet servicing both brothers.

They had identical dicks, but Arlo had shaved his bush and balls and Milo had gone all-natural. They tasted good and their lime and leather smell was intensified in their crotches. I sucked on one cock while I worked over the second one with my hand and then switched places. I eventually smashed both of their joints together so that I could suck them at the same time.

The boys had longer than average cocks and they were real thick. I thought about having them double penetrate me later, but I got the sense from them that they were uncomfortable with this much contact with the other, so I decided not to add to their stress. Several more seconds of each laphog brought them to their absolute hardest state.

I backed off of them and sat back on my heels as I looked up at the two brothers. It was disappointingly clear that neither of them had the gumption to command me the way

Gray did, so I crawled up onto the bed and waited for them.

I had not realized that I was waiting to be ordered around and I thought back fondly to Gray and the night we had spent together. It had been eye-opening for me and now I wasn't sure that anything else would live up to that one night.

Am I going to be constantly disappointed? Will I compare everything from here on out with that one night with Gray Carron?

Shocked to learn this about myself, I was flabbergasted that I craved someone to dominate me the way Gray had. I had always just assumed that I wanted to be in control of everything and now I was admitting the truth. It was like seeing the world for the very first time — everything was new and different.

Milo decided to go first, so he climbed onto the bed and I handed him a tube of lube. He squirted some on his hard cock as I pulled my legs back onto my chest and gave him a good view of his target. He did not use the lube on me, but he did spit onto my hole and pushed the loogie into me with the head of his slick dick.

"Fuck, that's tight," he told his brother as he pushed into me.

"Give it to him hard, Milo," Arlo encouraged his brother.

"Planning on it." Milo got into a comfortable position, pushing his weight down onto my folded thighs. He began to thrust and try to saw me in half until he ran out of steam and let his brother take over.

I could definitely get used to having two men servicing me, but there was an absence of heat from this fuck that bothered me. Both men were handsome and sexy. They were more than energetic enough to fuck me, but I still didn't feel what I wanted to experience.

"Bring that cock up here," I told Milo as he watched his brother rail me out.

He knelt beside my head and fed his long cock into my

mouth. I sucked on him while the matching pair probed my prostate repeatedly. The twins soon switched places and I took the opportunity to flip over onto all fours.

Milo used my hips to increase his speed and was soon buried to the root inside me. He dumped a big load of hot semen deep in my ass and Arlo took his place. The second brother churned the butter until he lost his shit and filled me with his seed also.

"Need a break or can you go again?" I asked the brothers as I reached for my glass on the nightstand.

"A small breather, please," Arlo said as he lay on his back on the bed breathing heavily.

I chuckled and chastised myself for being spoiled by Gray — the four-hour man. I crawled off the bed, went to the armoire and opened it. I had a huge TV facing the bed, so I turned it on and hit the play button on the DVD player.

Quickly, the picture on the screen changed from a commercial to a scene of fucking involving bondage with multiple marked men and NOMARs. I turned to look at Milo and Arlo.

"Just something to inspire you," I told them with a raised eyebrow.

There was a sling in the video and I figured that the boys were probably taking notes on how the actors were using it. The fucking in the video was especially hard and aggressive, and it seemed to have the desired effect I wanted it to have on the brothers.

Both of their cocks were twitching and starting to swell with blood again. It wouldn't be long now. I climbed onto the bed and sucked their cummy cocks back up to raging status again as they stared, drooling at the screen. I climbed on top of Arlo and straddled him. His slick cock easily found its way back into my tight hole.

I placed my palms flat down onto Arlo's magnificent pecs

and bounced myself up and down on his pogo stick. The bearded twin started to moan under me just as I moved over to his brother and repeated myself. Milo took over, put his hands on my hips, spread my butt cheeks apart, and began to fuck up into me from below.

Now, I was the one who was moaning. "Carry me to the sling, Milo," I commanded.

Milo responded by burying his prick deep inside me, holding my back with his arms, and sliding off the bed. He stood up, lifting me with him, and carefully walked towards the sling where he lay me down. Milo used the sling to move my ass back and forth so quickly on his long pole that my ass started to burn from the friction.

This party was just beginning.

CHAPTER SEVEN

A text string between Sutton Pike and his best friends the next day:

How were the bartenders, Sutton?
Not bad.
That's not a very glowing recommendation . . .
They took my mind off of other things . . .
Like what?
You have hot twins fucking you and you're still not satisfied?
I'm not sure what's wrong with me . . .
You'll know him when you meet him
I think I might have already . . .
The Romanian ambassador?
He's the American ambassador to Romania . . .
What are you going to do?
I've decided to go see him
Over there?
Of course. Wanna go?
Fuck yes!
Yes!
Romania, here we come!

Adam, Justin, and I made our plans very quickly. Adam lived in California and Justin lived in Virginia, so we agreed to meet in DC and catch a plane to Romania via New York. They would come to my apartment next week and we would leave shortly thereafter.

We were fortunate to be wealthy, thanks to our time in The Service. That was extremely helpful to someone like me who wanted to fly to Eastern Europe at the drop of a hat and spend two weeks touring the country.

It was an exciting prospect and I couldn't wait for it to begin. I was overcome with joy that I was going to get to see Romania and my cock was in a constant state of agitation at the prospect of bending to Gray's will.

How in the world had my life gone in this direction? The very thing that I always thought was my greatest strength was turning out to be what was keeping me from being truly happy.

Needing to call Gray and tell him the news, I quickly calculated the seven-hour time difference between our two countries. Figuring that I was okay at this time of day, I pulled up his contact and pressed the call button.

"Hi there," he said with a strange mixture of excitement and dread to his voice.

"Hey."

"I'm glad you called me, Sutton." His voice was absolutely smoldering with lust even through the phone.

"I called you with some good news," I teased him.

"If you were my pet, you wouldn't be allowed to keep secrets from me," he said firmly.

"I'm telling you now," I protested, already feeling a little flustered by his command of me. The tingle in my balls had turned into a full-scale electrical storm that was going to have my cock hard in just a second.

Gray Carron made a small humming noise and then said, "I don't hear you telling me anything yet."

"Sorry, I'm trying," I said quickly. "I'm coming to Romania," I blurted out before he could say anything else to me.

"Fuck me!" he said excitedly.

"You didn't expect me to come?"

Gray ignored my question and asked one of his own, "Is it a visit or a move?"

I swallowed hard because this was the part that I didn't think he was going to be happy with at all. "Two of my friends are going to join me for the first two weeks and then they will leave."

"And you will stay?" He sounded hopeful.

"For at least three months, Gray, and then I will decide what I want to do."

"It will be a trial?"

"Yes, it will be a trial. We will be a trial," I corrected him.

"Very well. I will have to make it nice and comfortable for my pet so that he wants to stay with his Master."

"That would be nice."

"What will be nice is when you are firmly impaled on my cock and completely at my command."

I was at a loss for words.

My silence didn't seem to upset Gray in any way. He ordered, "Tell me when you will come to me, Sutton."

"Well, I was hoping to come next week, if that is okay with your calendar. I know it is short notice, Gray."

"It will be fine. The sooner I can have you here, the sooner you will be pinned beneath me and unable to resist."

Fuck me! This man is really pouring it on. For the first time in my life, I was putty in a NOMAR's hands. It was not a comfortable position for me to be in, but it turned me on like almost nothing else ever had.

"Are you sure, Gray?" I asked, holding my breath. I didn't want him to change his mind, but I felt like I had to ask.

"I am sure. I will provide you with tourist visas and my security detail will keep you safe while you are here."

"That is most generous of you. And is the embassy big

enough for us to crash?

"We will make it work. And how will you keep yourself safe until you reach me?"

I explained that we were going to hire two bodyguards to accompany us.

"That is smart, Sutton. You will call me tomorrow with the flight details. Do you understand, pet?"

"Yes, Sir."

"Good. You've made me very happy tonight, my pet. I look forward to our reunion."

I could tell from his voice that he was being honest with me. "Me too, Gray. You sure I won't be a distraction to you?"

"Oh, I'm sure that you will be a distraction, pet. In fact, I am counting on it. Now, go make your travel arrangements to come to me."

"Yes, Sir. Goodnight."

"Goodnight, Sutton."

I had to admit that I was more than just a little excited. Gray and I had decided that my friends and I would come for a visit for two weeks and then Adam and Justin would leave, and I would stay for three months. After that time period, I would decide whether to continue in Romania with Gray or be done with him and return to America.

I masturbated as soon as I disconnected the phone call. My release came hard and fast, and I was completely wiped out afterwards. Gray was doing things to me that I didn't even know were possible. His command of me was so unexpected and wonderful.

On Sunday, I called my father and we had a very long talk. He was used to me traveling since I had left The Service but being so far away and for so long was not something with which he was entirely comfortable. We discussed my safety in Romania, Gray Carron, and the political stability of the region. I could tell that he didn't want me to go but was too proud to say it.

On Monday, I met with my banker, Henderson, who was also a close friend of mine. Preston had introduced us and he also used him for all of his investments and banking needs. Henderson assured me that as much money as I would need would be available to me while I was in Eastern Europe. He also assured me that he would keep careful tabs on everything while I was gone and would report to me each week. Preston promised me that he wouldn't let one penny of my hard-earned money get out of his hands and that I would have more money when I returned than I did when I left.

Tuesday, I had dinner with Preston and went over all of my travel plans with him. He was very supportive and approved of all the moves that I had made. I told him that I would check in with him often. I also asked him to keep an eye on Henderson and my money, which he agreed to do.

By the middle of the week, I met with the security agency that I had hired to accompany us. The manager came to my apartment with the two ex-Seals that had been chosen for our assignment. They went over what I wanted from them for the trip and took notes on everything I said. They promised me that they would develop the security protocols based on what I had told them and would be back Friday to go over them with me. I was impressed with their professionalism and I made sure to tell them that on their way out. I asked their boss to give me a moment alone.

"Mr. Hudson, I can't help but notice that the two men that you have chosen for this assignment are fucking hot as hell," I said to the manager once we were alone.

"Are they?" he asked evasively.

I nodded my head firmly. "They are."

"Luke and Cameron are our two best assets."

I made a small noise of conciliation. "We will just have to

deal with them on Friday."

"What does that mean?"

"My friends will be here on Friday, and we will have to get fucked by these two to get it out of the way." I would enjoy the looks on the two muscular giants' faces when I got to tell them.

Mr. Hudson looked non-plussed. "I'm afraid that will be against the rules, Mr. Pike."

"I'm sure that your men are supposed to follow the client's orders."

"To a degree," he carefully said.

"Well, I'm telling you that I won't be able to concentrate until I get railed out by them and they are probably the same way. So, it has to be done."

"Better here than on the actual assignment, I guess," Mr. Hudson finally acquiesced.

"Yes," I agreed as I walked to the door and opened it. "See you on Friday, boys," I told the ex-military men waiting outside my door.

The ex-Seals had shit-eating grins on their faces when they left my apartment that day after I told them my plans. I can only assume that they were looking forward to Friday just like I was.

Having everything in order made me feel better about the whole trip. I bought the airline tickets later that afternoon. This was really going to happen and I couldn't wait for the week to end so that it could start. Adam and Justin were due to arrive on Friday morning.

CHAPTER EIGHT

An excerpt of the Wikipedia page of Gray Carron

Born: January seventh, nineteen eighty-one
Residence: Hartford, Connecticut
College: BS from Dartmouth; MBA from Rutgers
Occupation Co-owner, Carron Investments
Co-owner, Carron Shipping
Owner, Gray Carron Holdings, Inc.
Years active: Two thousand to present
Net worth: US $200 Million
Parents: Ian Carron, father
Birthmother: Unknown
Relatives: Humbert Carron, grandfather
Alistar Carron, great-grandfather
Poole and Peake Carron, twin brothers
Public Image: GOP Chair, Chesterton County, Connecticut
Mercy General Hospital, Board of Directors
Carron Scholarship, Trustee
Master, numerous Servants

I picked Adam up from Dulles International on Friday morning. I had Justin with me already since he had driven up from Richmond an hour earlier. The three of us easily fell back into our old friendship, talking and laughing like we had never been away from each other. It was like we were right back at the SA again.

Adam had enough luggage for several months abroad and Justin and I made sure we gave him crap for it. I had rented a car for the weekend and now I was thinking that I needed to have rented one with a larger trunk.

I told the boys that I had a surprise for them after lunch and then drove them to DuPont Circle to eat at a place called Annie's Paramount Grill. It was one of my favorite restaurants in DC, and I was going to really miss it once we were in Europe.

I had purposely kept the details of my conversation with Gray quiet, so that I could tell my best friends the story in person. Over lunch, I recounted some of the things that he had said to me and admitted to Justin and Adam how much his words excited me.

Both Justin and Adam had been blessed with really good Masters who knew how to command, so they were happy for me that I was going to get to experience that with Gray. I couldn't wait for them to meet him and hear their opinions on him afterwards.

"So, what is our surprise?" Adam asked as we rode the elevator up to my apartment. Adam was just as handsome as he had been in school—thin and athletic with dark hair and substantial stubble on his face.

"Yeah, Sutton. What are you holding out on us?" Justin had changed a lot since school. His body had been doughy in school, but now he was toned and developed like a model. His Master had done wonders in getting him into shape. His blond hair was cut short in a military style and his smooth-shaven face always held a mischievous grin.

"You'll see," I said mysteriously as I used my key to enter my apartment. I was helping Adam with some of his luggage, which I put down directly in my spare room.

My two friends looked around my place, making comments about my style and pictures, while I poured us all a glass of champagne. "Let's toast to the trip," I said as I raised my glass.

"Here, here," Justin said, taking a glass and clinking mine. Adam did the same.

Just as I enjoyed my first sip of the expensive bubbly, the intercom buzzed. "Ah, here comes the surprise."

I buzzed the security guards up and opened the door for them.

"There is no better way for us to begin our adventure than with a little party with two former Navy Seals," I told my best friends as the two security guards entered the apartment.

"Whoa," Adam said as he saw the two hulking bodies fill up the space in my living room. Adam, like me, had a real thing for big guys, so I knew he was mentally picturing himself under them right now.

"Jesus," Justin said shortly thereafter. He had an affinity for black men and one of the guards sent by the security agency was a big, beautiful, bald man who was as black as he was hot.

I shut the door and locked it. "Boys, why don't you introduce yourselves?"

"I'm Hawkes," the brown-haired piece of muscle said.

"Edgerton," the bald one said in a super-deep voice that made Justin visibly quiver.

"I'm Sutton," I said, grinning broadly.

"Jason."

"Adam," my friend said with a small wave.

Hawkes was carrying a folder with my name on it, so I asked for it. It was the outline of the security protocol for the trip. I asked a few questions while Adam poured the two big men some champagne. They answered my questions quickly and with no hesitation, so I was satisfied.

"Now, fellas," I addressed them holding up my glass.

"This party is a one-time thing just to cut the sexual tension between the five of us. Do you understand?"

"Yes," Edgerton said.

"Yes."

"Good. And this is something that you both want, yes?"

"Hell, yes!" Hawkes said quickly. "I've never met anyone like you who just said what you wanted right up front and made it happen."

"It's just the way he is, Hawkes," Justin told him making an overly exaggerated eye roll.

"You will get used to it," Adam added dryly.

"Edgerton?" I prompted him.

"I am at your service, Sir," he said with a slight bow of his head.

"It's good to be on the other side," I said with a laugh. "Our excitement to fuck with you today does not give you permission to force yourself on us at any time later. If one of us would like to repeat the . . . experience with one or more of you, we will let you know. Understand?"

"Yes, Sir," they both answered.

"Excellent," I said, not only because they understood the rules, but because I had been able to establish that I was in command and there would not be any leeway in that.

"I hope you boys have good stamina," Justin said as he dropped to his knees and began to undo the military belt of Edgerton. He turned to me and said, "Paul is going to kill me."

"Alan, also," Adam chimed in.

"Oh, please," I said dismissively. "Your boyfriends will be having just as much fun while you are away as we are having."

"I kinda doubt that." Adam easily stripped Hawkes' pants and underwear down to the top of his military boots.

Edgerton's cock was revealed to be a long beauty with

average girth while Hawkes had an average length dick that was fat and veiny. Put them together and they could satisfy anyone's itch.

I opened the French doors to the bedroom and stripped off all of my clothes, being careful to let both Navy men get a good look at my ass as I bent to take my socks off. I put on quite the show for them while my two best friends were slobbing their knobs. Hawkes and Edgerton both took their khaki canvas shirts off, revealing rippling, muscled chests.

I joined Adam kneeling on the floor in front of Hawkes. I was soon sucking that fat rod while Adam got nude. I sucked Hawkes' big ball sack into my mouth while I held his thick joint up to his hairy belly while I watched Justin lead the big black security guard to my bed.

"Mind if I steal him, Sutton?"

"Not at all," I said, wiping my mouth.

A naked Adam was soon pulling Hawkes towards the bedroom. I got up from my knees, grabbed several bottles of water and joined everyone in the bedroom.

Edgerton had Justin bent over the side of the bed and was fucking him like he just got released from prison. Adam lubed up Hawkes' baby arm before he lay down on the bed on his back and pulled his legs up to his chest.

I knelt on the bed in front of Justin's head and the former Servant seamlessly sucked my big cock into his mouth without interrupting Edgerton's thrusts in the slightest. His hot mouth felt just as good as I remembered it and both of us were moaning before long.

Hawkes fed his thick prick into Adam's hole and announced, "Holy Fuck, Ed! This one has a tight little hole."

"This one is milking me like one of those machines back on the dairy farm when I was a kid," his fellow ex-Seal said.

"His mouth is pretty fucking hot, as well," I chimed in. "I better check this one's out, just to be fair." I moved over to

Adam's head and dipped my cock down into his open mouth like I was making a bees' wax candle. "Just as good," I commented immediately.

It was more than fun to watch my two favorite people in the world getting railed out by two big NOMARs, and to have them sucking my dick at the same time was just over-the-top. I vowed to show them a good time while the three of us were in Romania. I figured that I would be caught up in the irresistible vortex that was Gray Carron's personality, but I didn't want that to take time away from Justin and Adam. It would be hard for me, but I was determined to make it work.

Edgerton pulled his hard cock out of Justin and raised an eyebrow at me. I climbed onto Justin's back, straddling his butt and then placed my crotch down onto the small of his back. Now, Edgerton had two holes lined up and I didn't need to explain to him what to do next.

The security guard pushed his cock head against my puckered hole until it popped inside. His cock snaked its way down my anal channel until it finally hit the bottom. Edgerton fucked me hard and deep for a few strokes before he removed it and slammed it into Justin's ass again. He went back and forth four or five times before he busted his nut in my friend's ass.

Hawkes must have come at almost the same exact moment, because he was practically lying on top of little Adam and breathing like he had just run a five K.

"Gotta try these two," Edgerton told his buddy. "Sutton's ass was squeezing the shit out of me and then you think you're going to get some relief and his buddy is the milking machine."

I couldn't help but laugh which caused everyone else to do the same.

Hawkes pushed himself up with his big biceps, pulled his

dick out of Adam, and said, "It's our goddamn lucky day, Ed."

"You can say that again," his friend said back as they switched places.

I slid to the side off of Justin and flipped him over onto his back. "I think you are mistaken about who is having the lucky day, gentlemen." I flipped around so that my mouth was lined up with Justin's hole as my head hung slightly off the edge of the bed.

"Agreed," Justin said.

"For sure," Adam confirmed.

Hawkes mounted my mouth, giving me a cum-sickle to suck on as he said, "I guess we will just have to keep going to see who is right."

Fucking A!

CHAPTER NINE

Part of a text string between Sutton Pike and Gray Carron on Sunday, May second:

How are you today, my pet?
I'm good . . . u?
I'm excited about you coming to me tomorrow
Me too!
Have you had fun with Justin and Adam?
Oh yeah!
My pet does enjoy having his asshole stretched out, doesn't he?
I do . . .
I will keep it stretched to its limits . . .
Promise?
Have no fear!
I'll hold you to that
Text me when you land in Russia tomorrow
Yes, Sir
And Sutton . . .
Yes, Sir?
Don't keep me waiting

The things that Gray said made my blood boil and my heart raced the closer I got to him. My flight on the Russian airline, Aeroflot, connected through Moscow and we had an eight-hour layover. The ten-hour flight had been hard on my big frame and I was grateful for the reprieve when we could finally de-board.

Justin, Adam, and I had flown first class, so we had to wait on Edgerton and Hawkes to catch up with us from coach once we were released into the airport. The three of us spent the waiting time talking about all the freaks whom we had just been stuck with inside a metal tube for the last ten hours.

Our bodyguards joined us shortly. The two big ex-seals couldn't resist the urge to exaggeratedly twist their necks and rub their thighs. They had not been happy to ride coach while we were in first class, but neither of them seemed to have the nerve to say anything directly to us about it.

"What took you so long?" I smirked at them.

"Yeah, don't keep us waiting next time, fellas," Adam said, tongue-in-cheek.

Justin asked, "How was coach?"

"Small," Edgerton croaked.

"Let's stretch your legs out by starting to walk." I turned to take the long hallway down to customs.

It was a huge hallway that wound around the airport—upstairs and then back down them, through doors that led to more hallways, and past no one. The long line of the same people who had been on the plane with us continued down the path.

Customs was a very small glass booth that we could only approach one at a time. A very large Russian man in a military uniform held us in check at a security line until the person in front of us was finished with the customs agent. There were still about six people in line ahead of us when the seemingly disinterested military guy spotted Justin, Adam, and I. His keen eyes seemed to appraise Hawkes and Edgerton behind us. I watched as he turned and spoke into a walkie-talkie on his uniform jacket.

"We've been noticed," I mumbled under my breath.

There were only one or two men whose smells had appealed to me while we were on the plane, so it pretty easy to resist, but I could smell this guy so strongly in my nostrils that I felt weak to ignore him.

"Yes," Justin said firmly.

Soon we had moved up by three people and a second military man appeared. The new arrival came over to talk to the man running the line, staring at Justin, Adam, and I the whole time. After several minutes, he motioned us through a separate line by removing the barricade temporarily.

"What's going on?" I asked the new guy.

"Security protocol," he told me in very stilted English.

The two guards ushered us into a holding chamber off to the side.

"This is not good," Hawkes said once the door was shut and we were alone in the room.

"They want to fuck," I said flatly.

"How do you know?" Edgerton asked, his eyes wide open.

I rolled my eyes at our security team. "Because that is what all NOMARs want."

"We will see what they say. They are coming back now," Adam said.

The security guards now numbered three and they motioned for our guards to come with them after opening the door. Hawkes and Edgerton followed the Russians to a glass cell right beside ours.

"Well, that just proves that I'm right," I said.

"Yes," Adam agreed.

The Russians were back at our cell and the one in charge said, "Strip search."

I looked at my friends. "Should we comply?"

"They are cute," Adam said.

"You're just turned on by how big they are," Justin told

him.

Adam quickly asked, "So?"

I turned to the officers. "After we fuck around with you, you will let us leave?"

The alpha male grinned broadly. "But, of course."

"We have your word of honor?"

"Yes," they all agreed.

I looked at Adam and Justin and we agreed nonverbally. With a quick wink to our security guards in the cell beside us, I started to take my clothes off and my friends followed suit. We were soon on our knees on the hard concrete floor sucking cock.

All three men had decent dicks and were freshly showered, so the experience was not bad. I just didn't like that they never took off their clothes during the whole thing, but I understood their need for speed. What they were doing was highly illegal and unethical, so they didn't want to get caught.

Each one of the Russian military men fucked us. They took turns thrusting their sausages into us and then would all switch at the same time, like we were on a conveyor belt of sex. I enjoyed being fucked even more than the next guy, but this screw left me feeling unsatisfied and bothered. I hated having sex with clothing on—it made me feel slutty and disconnected.

Each of the three men blew their loads in one of our asses and then high-fived their co-workers. They thanked us, released us from the cell, and showed us where there was a bathroom in which we could clean up afterwards. I demanded that the military men release our security guards first and they complied.

"Fucking red bastards," Hawkes said as he stood against the inside of the bathroom door while Justin, Adam, and I washed ourselves.

"Don't be so narrow-minded to think that the American customs agents wouldn't do the same thing, Hawkes," I admonished him. "Because they would in a heartbeat."

"I guess it's more that I don't like being helpless to protect you," Hawkes admitted.

Justin said, "I appreciate that, but we were okay."

Edgerton said, "Never-the-less, I can't wait until they give me my gun back."

We all chuckled as we left the bathroom and finally went through customs the right way. The Russian officers on duty now acted like they were hardly aware of us, and not as if they had just partied with us. Most people would have been annoyed by that, but I appreciated it.

My group stepped out into the terminal directly into a crush of people—most of whom were Asian or Russian. They looked and dressed like most Americans and I was surprised that the restaurants and shops dotting the sides of the building were mostly American businesses.

"Anyone hungry?" the big Edgerton asked. His dark skin made him stick out like a sore thumb in the crowd of white people. We had already learned that this security guard had a bottomless pit for a stomach.

"I could eat," I said as I took a step forward.

Suddenly, a man dressed like a peasant darted out of the crowd right at me. Hawkes pulled me back to the side, but the stranger came right after me and pointed at my chest with a bony finger. He looked old but probably wasn't as old as he looked. His skin and clothes were dirty and he smelled like boiled cabbage.

"*Catalizator!*" he screamed at me.

"What?" I looked from my friends to my bodyguards. The expressions on their faces were ones of confusion, which was exactly how I felt.

"*Catalizator!*" the old man screeched again, before quickly covering his mouth with his hand and darting his eyes from side to side.

I again looked at my travelling companions and they shrugged back to me just as the old man faded back into the crowd.

"What the fuck?" I asked.

Justin asked, "What was he yelling?"

"None of us speak Russian," Adam said, stating the obvious.

"We can ask at the restaurant." I started to walk out into the terminal again. "Anybody hungry for anything in particular?"

"Italian," Justin yelled from the back of our party.

I headed down the terminal towards a large restaurant called Roma. We were seated and had ordered when I asked the question of the waiter. "Do you know what the word *catalizator* means?"

The waiter shook his head. "It is not Russian."

"It's not?" I asked in confusion.

He shook his head side to side, smiled, and headed towards the kitchen.

Adam held up his phone and announced, "I just Google translated it, Sutton. It doesn't come up with anything."

Thankfully, nothing else unusual happened to us in the Moscow Airport that day. I called Gray and he sounded so pleased that I was almost to him that I even forgot about the old man yelling at me. My travelling companions and I spent the rest of the layover shopping and charging our phones at our gate. Romania was just three hours away, and my body was starting to vibrate with my nervous energy.

Edgerton and Hawkes whined as Adam, Justin, and I were called to take our seats in first class. Later, when the two big bodyguards were allowed to board, they glared at us as they headed back to coach. I felt sorry for the big guys, but they were right behind us in the first row of business class.

The flight to Romania was spent in a fitful sleep for me. I feel asleep almost as soon as we took off. Normally, I would be unable to sleep on a plane, but my nervous energy seemed to have had the opposite effect on me.

I dreamt that I was standing in a small clearing in the woods. The moon was right over my shoulder—big and full like a spotlight. I got the impression that there was something in the woods, but I couldn't quite see what it was.

I watched the woods and breathed in deeply of the night air. Something moved in front of me in the foliage. Suddenly, I heard voices behind me and the creature in the woods howled in pain. The voices all turned to howls that faded into the night. The soft hoots of an owl were the only sound I could hear now.

I woke with a start and a throbbing headache. The seat in front of me had a flight tracker monitor on it that revealed that we were right on the border of Romania. My adventure was beginning, but I felt like my head was about to explode.

Chapter Ten

A quiz on Romania found in the Aeroflot onboard magazine in the seat pocket of first class:

Q. What US state is the same size as Romania?
A. Michigan
Q. What is Romania's chief export?
A. Cars
Q. What is the Romanian currency called?
A. Leu or Lei
Q. Romania's largest city?
A. Bucharest
Q. Romania has sixty percent of which of Europe's native wildlife?
A. Brown bears
Q. Percentage of the population that identifies as Gypsy?
A. Twelve percent
Q. Famous Romanians?
A. Vlad the Impaler (Dracula), Nadia Comaneci (gymnast), Johnny Weissmuller (Tarzan)
Q. What sea borders Romania to the East?
A. Black Sea

Our plane landed and I had already taken three extra-strength Tylenol for my headache. I was feeling better, but there was still a buzzing in my head that I was not used to feeling. I dug my sunglasses out of my carry-on and put them over my eyes.

My sunglasses did not hide me from an attack by a family of Gypsies as soon as we left the confines of the airport. This family included an older man, a young man, and two really small boys. They looked clean and well-dressed.

The older man pointed right at me and yelled, "*Catalizator!*"

"Again? Really?" I asked in frustration.

"Why are they always pointing at you?" Justin asked.

Hawkes and Edgerton stepped between me and the family. The Gypsies were rattling on excitedly in a language that I assumed was Romanian while looking right at me. They had moved closer but stopped when our bodyguards formed a shield. The family soon moved away from us, the older man still yelling the now-familiar word at me.

We had caused quite a commotion at the airport. Adam took advantage of the gathering crowd to ask a young man who looked like he might be in college, "Hey, do you know what the word *catalizator* means in English?"

He smiled and answered, "It means *catalyst*."

"Catalyst?" Justin asked. "What does that mean?"

Adam was already Googling it. "Something that speeds up a chemical reaction without changing itself."

"Why would they yell that at me?" I asked, suddenly holding my head again against the buzzing.

Adam understood that I wasn't feeling well, so he took over control—picking up our luggage, finding our way to the bank where we could convert our dollars into Romanian leis, finding us a taxi, and communicating with the driver to take us to the American embassy.

The ride through Bucharest was cool. The city was very old-world European with modern commerce sprinkled between wooded parks. Some of the buildings looked like they were built during the communist occupation—very militaristic and boxy looking.

The cab soon stopped in a trendy area downtown on a tree-lined street. I saw the American flags flying before we even came to a stop. The tingling in my balls immediately began. I guessed that I was less than a thousand feet from Gray.

Adam paid the cab driver who unloaded our luggage onto the sidewalk before pulling away. I told the guys to wait here with our stuff. I walked up to the gate of the embassy and pressed the button for the intercom.

"Yes?" an American voice answered.

"Hello," I said. "Sutton Pike to see the Ambassador."

"Welcome to Romania, Mr. Pike. Someone will be right down for you in a minute."

"Thank you," I said before rejoining my party on the sidewalk.

After a minute, the front door opened and a tall, thin man emerged and came down the stairs. He stopped at the security gate, spoke to the guards, and the gate slowly opened.

"Is that him?" Justin whispered to me.

"No," I said flatly. I did not know this man in the expensive, ill-fitting suit walking towards us.

"Mr. Pike?" the young man asked, looking between me and my two marked friends.

"Yes," I answered cautiously.

He smiled and shook my hand. "So, nice to meet you, Mr. Pike. I'm Craig, Mr. Carron's personal assistant."

"Nice to meet you."

"The Ambassador apologizes for his absence, Mr. Pike, but he is in a meeting that he could not reschedule."

I was disappointed. Gray had been given plenty of notice.

Craig swallowed hard and suddenly looked uncomfortable. "He has asked me to show you to your rooms." He pointed across the street behind us.

I looked over my shoulder and then back to Craig. "I thought we were staying in the embassy, Craig."

Craig started to move towards the street. "Mr. Carron thought you might be more comfortable here."

"Lead the way," I finally said.

The hotel across the street from the embassy was ultra-modern and high class. Gray had reserved four rooms for us on the top floor. The rooms were together, each one bigger than the next and some of them overlooking the embassy. I looked down at the ornate building and wondered if Gray was looking at the hotel right now.

Justin, Adam, and I each took one of the hotel rooms and left the last one for our bodyguards to share. Their room was conveniently located right across the hall from the three of ours.

My headache had not gone away, but it had been reduced to a dull throb. I took some more Tylenol. "And how long will the ambassador be in his meeting, Craig?"

Craig looked like he had eaten something sour. "He should be . . . available by some point after dinner."

The rest of my group was still gathered in my sitting room. I turned to them. "Well, boys, where shall we go to have dinner?"

"I'm tired," Adam admitted. "I would be okay eating here at the hotel and getting to bed early."

"I'm for that," Justin chimed in.

"Then that's what we shall do. Craig, please inform Mr. Carron that we will be in for the night. Maybe we will see him in the morning," I said with biting sarcasm.

"Yes, sir. Nice to meet you, sir." Craig looked at me like one would a cobra before leaving my room.

Our party of five were soon showered and seated at a large table in the hotel restaurant. The menu was surprisingly American with some Romanian specials added. I had the pastrami since it was the specialty of the house. It was roasted pork with polenta which was quite delicious.

Justin flirted with our waiter and slipped him his room key after we paid the bill. Adam and I kidded with him, but in seriousness, I asked Hawkes and Edgerton to please stay up and check on him if they could. Our safety was my highest priority on this night.

Hawkes made sure I was in for the night before he left my room for his. I turned on the TV but muted it. The window seemed to hold my attention and I stood in front of it for some little time watching the lit windows of the American embassy.

I was still standing looking out the window when he appeared at my door. Smelling him before actually seeing him, I debated with myself about whether to go jerk the door open or not. I didn't have to decide because I soon heard the key card reader click, and the door to my room swung open.

I hesitated for a second but did not turn around. "Gray."

"Pet," Gray said in his deep, lust-filled voice. I turned around and looked directly into his eyes. Those dark eyes locked onto mine and held me as easily as if he had reached inside my chest and wrapped his hand around my heart.

Gray had recently showered and shaven, by the smell of him. That seemed odd since he was coming from a meeting.

"Are you mad at me, my pet?" he asked in an almost whisper.

"Irritated more than mad," I answered a little too quickly.

"I apologize for that, but I am thrilled to see you here."

"Thank you for the rooms."

"You're welcome." He paused and there was an uncomfortable silence between us. I watched as Gray suddenly set his jaw and then said, "We need to fuck—hard and fast. Then we will be more relaxed and can talk."

I nodded my agreement.

"Kneel," Gray ordered while pointing to the carpet in front of him.

I was drawn to this man like no other, but as I knelt in front of him and unzipped the fly of his dress pants, I started to question it. I didn't question the lust I had for him or the way both of our bodies overheated when we were together. Neither did I question his fucking ability or his ability to dominate me.

Am I going to let Gray do whatever he wants where I'm concerned? Is he going to be able to treat me like shit and then just show up with his undeniable masculine appeal and make it all better? Well, maybe I can just let him take advantage of me this one time . . .

I reached into Gray's fly, wrapped my fingers around his big laphog, and pulled it carefully out. I had forgotten how magnificent that hot piece of meat was until I had my hand wrapped around it and was guiding it towards my mouth. His cock was so hot that it felt like it might burn me.

The Ambassador's skin tasted clean, so I ran my tongue all over the soft head and shaft of his cock while my lips stretched wide. The soft cock head of Gray Carron punched into the back of my throat as my lips and tongue stretched forward to the root of his big tree. I breathed in deeply of his masculine scent as my nose buried in his pubic hair. The smell of firewood and apples was overwhelming in my sinus cavity.

I sucked his cock with long, drawing pulls that hollowed out my cheeks. Increasing my speed, I could feel Gray getting close to his release. He put a hand on the top of my head.

"You do something to me, pet," he groaned as he hit the top stair of the ladder.

I sucked hard one more time before just keeping his super-soft cock head in my mouth and nibbled on it. Gray came immediately, shocking me with the intensity of his orgasm. I swallowed fast to keep from choking but still wound up with trails of hot cum pouring out of the sides of my mouth.

Wrapping my hand around the bottom of Gray's shaft, I licked his cock clean before sitting back onto my haunches and looking up at him.

"Thank you, my pet," Gray said as he looked intently down at me.

"Welcome, sir."

"Are you ready to get fucked hard, Sutton?"

"Yes, sir."

"Okay, then. No more words out of your pie hole, understand?"

I nodded instead of answering.

"Oh, you make me very hot for you, my pet."

I want you to fuck me hard, Gray.

The new ambassador to Romania looked down at me and ordered, "Take my tie off, pet."

I did, reaching up high to work the knot down before I could pull the silk through his shirt collar and into my hand. I had a pretty good idea what Gray was going to do with that tie and my hard cock sticking me in the stomach told me that it already knew also.

"Hands above your head, pet. Interlock your fingers for me."

I followed his instructions, getting more excited the more he commanded me.

"Where shall we fuck, my pet?"

My eyes involuntarily darted to the window. There was still something there that was drawing me, even though this gorgeous, sexy man was standing right before me undressing. I had previously come to the conclusion that Gray's presence across the street was what was drawing my attention to the window, but now that he was here, I had to reconsider.

He followed my split-second eye movement towards the window with his own eyes. "The window?" His face broke into a huge grin, and he bound my wrists with one end of his tie. He pulled on the other end of the tie, causing me to scramble to my feet.

Gray walked me over to the window and threaded his end of the tie through the curtain rod and pulled it tight. It made me stand right up against the window and stretch to the curtain rod.

"Good choice, my pet. We shall fuck where all of Bucharest can watch us."

CHAPTER ELEVEN

Part of a letter written by Sutton Pike to his father on May sixteenth from Bucharest, Romania, mailed later that day:

Hi Dad,

Just wanted to drop you a letter today. I just dropped Justin and Adam off at the airport for their flight home and I'm back at the hotel feeling a little lonely now that they are gone.

We've had a great two weeks in Romania. This country is everything that I hoped it would be. I have tons of pictures and souvenirs to show you when I get home. My friends and I have toured every castle and the birthplace of Vlad Dracul. We toured from one end of the country to the opposite, swimming in the Black Sea and hiking in the Carpathian Mountains.

We toured a huge salt mine and rode on an underground Ferris wheel. I really enjoyed the day we spent boating on the Danube. Bucharest became our playground and I've loved every minute of it.

And, yes, Dad, I have been safe. My friends and I hired bodyguards as our constant companions. Edgerton is making the return trip home today with Adam and Justin, but Hawkes is staying here with me. Gray, the American ambassador, has offered to provide me with security while I am here, but for now I prefer to use my own.

Gray has not been so easy. He is far busier than I would like him to be. I don't get to see or spend much time with him, but am hoping now that my friends have gone home that it will change. If it doesn't change, then I will probably be coming home soon. Although to be quite honest with you, there is something here in Bu-

charest that has been affecting me – pulling me, drawing me here. It is something that I have never experienced before and it might be worth exploring.

Hawkes and I had moved into a suite in the hotel which was basically two bedrooms connected with a kitchen and a living room. It had a fantastic view of the front door of the embassy, but that building wasn't what usually drew my attention.

My headaches had never gone away. They were reduced to a slow throbbing that I had come to live with. Something in my gut told me that it was not a medical condition that I was suffering from, but I had no rational proof of that. There was something instinctual about it – something that kept me excited to be here and that kept my cock hard as a rock.

From this window, I had noticed that Craig, Gray's assistant, left the embassy every day at nine o'clock to get coffee from down the street. It was one minute before nine right now as I watched from the window. Hawkes was already waiting on the sidewalk outside the embassy.

The door to the embassy opened and Craig appeared right on time. As soon as he was through the security gate and onto the sidewalk, Hawkes was upon him. They talked briefly and then headed towards the front door of the hotel. It looked like Craig was not really coming of his own accord.

I only had to wait a minute before they appeared in the room in front of me. "Craig, how nice to see you again," I said to him with my best fake smile plastered on my face.

"Mr. Pike. Your . . . man was quite insistent that you needed to speak to me," Craig said to me nervously.

"And indeed I do, Craig. Would you like to sit?"

"No, thank you."

"Then I won't waste your time, Craig. Now that my friends have left to go home, I cannot deny what I suspect any longer."

Craig had the good character not to say anything.

I could see that I was going to have to convince the ambassador's assistant to want to give me the information that I sought. "Craig, I just want to have all the information so that I can make an informed decision about my future. You won't deny me that, will you?"

"I think it is only fair, Sutton, but I'm concerned how you will use the information that I give you."

"I have no desire to embarrass Gray or the embassy. I am not going to make a scene, if that is what you are worried about."

Craig seemed to relax as his shoulders dropped and his hands unclenched. I had him.

"I suspect that the ambassador has other interests, Craig."

"You would be correct, Mr. Pike."

"Sutton, please. So, Mr. Carron has a Servant in the embassy?" I asked, although I pretty much knew the answer already.

"He brought a Servant with him when he came from the States."

I nodded my head as I processed this information.

Craig continued, "And of course, there was the Romanian Servant that was left behind when the former ambassador expired."

"What?" I asked, shooting a quick look at Hawkes.

Craig suddenly realized that I had not suspected this information. "His name is Iancu and apparently he and Jacob have formed quite a bond."

"What does that mean?"

"They tend to tag team the ambassador," he said with chagrin.

"No wonder he's so tired," I smirked.

"Nothing against you, Sutton," Craig said. "I overheard

him telling the associate ambassador that you were the best fuck he had ever had. I guess with the new job and the two marked men at his . . . disposal, he doesn't have much time for you."

"No, he doesn't," I agreed. "Well, thank you for your honesty, Craig."

"Will you go home, Sutton?"

"Not just yet. I would like to talk to Gray at least once more and there are still some things that I need to explore here in Romania."

"I see. Well, good luck to you."

"Thanks." I opened the hotel room door and let him out.

"So, what do you want to do now?" Hawkes asked me after the door was closed again.

I looked at him closely and then answered, "I meant what I said, Hawkes. I know you may think I'm crazy, but there is something here—something that may be amazing. Let's look for a place of our own now that we don't need to be here."

"Will do," Hawkes agreed, taking a seat on one of the couches with his laptop.

By the end of the day, Hawkes had found us an apartment that we could rent by the month that was more central to the Old Town section of the city that I liked so much. Hawkes and I had eaten a pizza and salad for dinner at a local bar, and the meal was exactly what I wanted it to be. I was very happy with my trip to Romania so far, even with the disappointing news about Gray.

Now that I was sure that Gray was busy with other Servants and I had decided not to be his pet, I was starting to notice the men of Bucharest as well. Surprisingly to me, they were pretty hot. Most of them worked out, at least on their upper bodies and many of them were very handsome.

Hawkes had retired to his bedroom for the night once he had ascertained that I was not going back out. I was lying on my bed trying to figure out what the gnawing feeling in my stomach was and what I was going to do about it. The knock on the hotel room door was soft when it came.

I jumped up in surprise, but I could smell who it was through the door before I even approached it. The unmistakable smell of firewood and MacIntosh apples crept under the door-jam like a snake slithering into a bog.

"Gray," I said as I opened the door for him.

"My pet," he said with a smile. "May I come in?"

"Of course," I agreed, moving to the side so he could enter.

He walked into the room and when he saw that I was alone, he stood in front of the window and faced me. I was unsure if he was trying to remind me of my first night in Romania when he had hung me from the curtain rod or not, but my body responded immediately to him anyway.

He seemed a little flustered. "So, Craig said that he talked to you today."

"He did," I said, not letting him off the hook.

"What did he tell you?"

"He confirmed what I already knew, Gray."

He sighed and his shoulders slumped. "I thought so. I'm sorry, Sutton."

"Sorry for what, Gray?"

"For not being honest with you, for having a Servant when I purposely got you to come visit me, for not giving you the attention you deserve. You take your pick."

"I accept your apology." I took a seat in the armchair facing him.

"Why aren't you more upset?" he asked, seeming to be more curious than anything else.

"I'm not sure," I answered honestly. I watched him come and sit on the couch close to me. "I think I must be more mature now," I said, tongue-in-cheek.

He laughed. "I never thought you would come and when you did, I didn't know what to do."

"I understand."

"Are you going to go home now?"

"No. There is something here that interests me still, so I'm going to move to an apartment closer to town and explore a little bit."

The look on his face told me that he was shocked as hell. He had not seen that one coming. "So, we are good?" he asked in disbelief.

"I'm going to be exploring my options, Gray. And if you want to call me sometime or take me out to dinner or a show, I will certainly answer my phone," I said plainly.

"Oh," he said with genuine surprise. "What options do you have to explore, Sutton?"

"Quite a few, I think . . ."

"Are you doing this to punish me?" he asked innocently.

I laughed out loud, so hard that Hawkes opened his door and stuck his head out. "We're okay," I assured him. Once he was back in his room, I turned back to Gray. "I don't want to punish you, Gray. I came here because I thought you were going to be the man that I could spend the rest of my life with. But now that I see that you aren't, I'm ready to move on."

"How do you know that I'm not the one?"

"Because the fact that you didn't make me the priority tells me that it's not a good fit for either one of us, Gray."

He hung his head in shame. "I'm sorry about that."

"Nothing to be sorry about. I've found in my quest for my true Master that it either is or it isn't, but it's no one's fault."

Gray lifted his head and looked me in the eyes. "That's very nice of you to say, but I still feel bad."

"Don't, Gray. Do you still enjoy fucking with me?" I asked bluntly.

"Yes!"

"Then we can still enjoy that for a while longer while I'm here, yes?"

"Yes," he agreed, finally smiling.

"I'll let you know where Hawkes and I settle," I informed him.

"That sounds good. You know you can stay here and I'll pay."

"Thanks, but I'm good. Something is waiting out there for me, and I'm determined to find out what it is."

"I'm sure you will," he agreed.

CHAPTER TWELVE

Part of a text string between Sutton Pike and his two best
friends, Adam and Justin, on May eighteenth:

Sutton, how's it going?
Pretty well, thanks!
Did you have the talk with Gray?
I did. It went better than I thought it would
You fucked around with him after, didn't you?
Of course! I'm such a slut!!
You gonna stay?
At least for a little while.
*Hawkes and I moved into an apartment near Old Town a few
days ago . . .*
Wow! Not wasting any time . . .
Yeah, I had a pretty good time furnishing it.
*Hawkes and I are going to go out tonight to celebrate our new
start.*
Woo-Hoo!
Time to get lucky!
Luck . . . please. Like shooting fish in a barrel!
Good luck, Sutton. Stay safe!
Will do. Love you guys!

I would have to apologize to Hawkes when I saw him next. I
had been a real whore over the past two weeks—keeping my
bodyguard out at clubs all night, dragging men back to our
apartment to sleep with, and otherwise being a real douche

of a client to him.

It was early afternoon and I was still in bed with my man from last night. He had his back to me as he slept on his side and I was sitting with my back against the headboard. This man, whose name was Boris, I think, was an amazing fuck. He had mad skills that most NOMARs didn't have because they don't have much practice.

I had met Boris at a sports bar where he had gone to watch a soccer game. He was just my type—tall, dark hair, dark beard and mustache, muscled, and thick. He had a giant hairy chest that I lay under most of the night as he fucked me with a long, thick cock. He was hot-natured like me, which reminded me of Gray for a brief moment. Not only was his skin temperature hot, but his cum was almost scalding when it poured forth out of his big dick.

The next morning, my ass was still throbbing from his assault on me. It was still dark in my bedroom, thanks to the blackout shades I had installed when we moved in, even though it was early afternoon. I was enjoying a moment of quiet because I had awoken to notice that the buzzing in my head had stopped. Not wanting to waste a second of quiet time, I was answering emails and texting friends. I had gotten into a routine of getting up in the early morning hours when the buzzing was quiet and sleeping in the late afternoon when it was loud.

Finally, I had to get up to use the bathroom, walking gingerly so that my ass wouldn't hurt much. After some time cleaning up, I decided to make us some breakfast. As quietly as I could, I started to make egg in a basket and fried potatoes. I put the coffee maker to work.

Either the smell or the noise woke Boris, and I heard him roll out of bed.

"Morning," I said to him in English since I had still not been able to pick up simple Romanian phrases.

He grunted something at me as he stumbled to the bath-room. I plated the eggs, toast, and potatoes and set them on the table. The coffee was ready, so I was pouring that into cups when Boris emerged.

"Thanks for cooking," Boris said in a gruff morning voice as he approached the table.

"Welcome," I replied as I turned around with the two cups of coffee.

And that's when I dropped them. I was so shocked by the man standing in front of me that I lost all sense of myself.

"What's wrong?" he asked, but with all the slight varia-tions that led me to believe he knew exactly what was wrong.

This was not the same man that I had just spent the night with. I mean, it was, but it wasn't. He was still the same handsome man that I had picked up at the bar last night, but his beard and mustache were gone. He was not fresh-shaven but had a five o'clock shadow. He was also slightly shorter than my six-foot-three-inch frame when I know last night he had been taller. The massive, hairy chest that I had run my hands over all night long was now a smooth, muscular, av-erage-sized chest.

I bent down to pick up the coffee cups and wipe up the black liquid on the floor. Boris came over to help me. I no-ticed that his big sexy feet from last night were now just reg-ular feet.

Was I really drunk last night? Drunk enough to remember the whole night a completely different way? I don't think so. I remem-ber Boris' body in great detail, and I explored every bit of it last night. There is no way that I was wrong on so many things.

"I'm sorry," Boris said, suddenly. "I wasn't supposed to stay the night, but I felt you were somehow different."

I laughed out loud as I stared at him. "Different, me?"

"Yeah. There's something about you . . ."

"I think there is something about you," I said to him as I

turned to get two more mugs and fill them with coffee.

"I know, and I felt like you were one of us." He sat down at the table.

"Us?" I asked.

Boris raked his hand through his short hair, which had been longer last night. "I felt like we were friends or something. That we knew each other and not just in that way." He nodded at the bedroom with his head.

I sat down at the table across from him and looked at him intently. "You knew you were going to change and that is why you weren't supposed to stay the night?"

"I didn't say that," he said with a smile as he tore into the egg in the middle of his toast.

"What are you?" I asked, a little too quickly.

"I'm a man that got very lucky last night to have caught your eye, Sutton Pike." He finished his egg and toast and drank the strong black coffee in one huge gulp. "It was a night that I will never forget."

"And a morning that I'm sure I won't, either," I said with sarcasm.

"You should. It will be dangerous for you, if you do not."

"What does that mean?"

"Nothing. Just forget about me and go on with your life." He went back into the bedroom, pulled on his jeans, stepped into his shoes, and pulled his now looser t-shirt on over his head. I noticed that he had to use his belt on the last hole to keep his pants from falling off. "Maybe we will meet again someday?"

"Maybe," I said. "If I'm still alive."

He looked at me oddly and said, "Why wouldn't you be alive?"

"You said it would be dangerous if I didn't forget you," I explained like he was a child.

He smiled. "There are worse things than death, Sutton."

He came over and kissed me on each cheek after I had stood and added, "But your ass is something to keep living for!" Boris smacked me hard on my ass cheek, reminding me of our long night of fucking.

"See ya," I said flippantly to him as he reached the door.

"Later," the much-changed man from my bed said as he left my apartment.

Hawkes emerged from his bedroom a minute later. He looked like he had been up for a little while.

"I don't know how you can go without sleep like you do, Hawkes," I said to him as I held up a coffee mug to him.

"Me?" he asked in fake shock. "You are the one that barely slept last night."

"Sorry about that. I will be sleeping the rest of the day probably."

"No problem. I couldn't help but overhear part of your conversation this morning. What was that all about?" Hawkes and I had become more than just client and customer since we had spent so much time together. We both considered each other friends and therefore this question was not completely out-of-line.

I was about to answer when a searing pain shot through my brain. I held my head on each side with my hands and collapsed onto the floor. Just as suddenly as it came, the pain left but was replaced with a voice. It was Boris' voice, but he didn't seem to be talking to me. It was hazy and distant and I was too shocked to even comprehend what the voice was saying.

How the hell is he doing this? Who is this man?

"Are you okay, Sutton?" Hawkes asked as he bent over me.

"I'm fine, I think."

"What is it?"

"I'm not sure," I said, listening intently but not hearing anything. Then the voice was back, but it was different. This was a different voice and he seemed to be answering Boris. These two men were having a conversation inside my head or I was seriously mentally ill.

I looked at Hawkes and said, "I have to lie down."

He picked me up in his powerful arms and carried me to my disheveled bed that still smelled like cum and man sweat. He placed me down gently and covered me up. "Aspirin?"

"No, thanks. I want to see how this plays out."

Hawkes looked confused, but I shut my eyes and tried to be still and quiet so that I could hear what was happening inside my skull. Unfortunately, all was silent, so I soon drifted off to sleep instead of gathering any more insight into my condition.

I was aware of Hawkes checking on me a couple of times throughout the afternoon and evening. I dreamed of foggy rooms with faceless men speaking to me and about me. I woke up feeling hung-over.

Hawkes was watching TV and playing solitaire on his laptop when I stumbled out of bed. Suddenly, I blurted out, "Wanna go to a soccer game tonight, Hawkes?" I wasn't even sure of where that idea came from now that I had voiced it.

"Fuck, yes!" he said without even looking up. "You feeling up to it?"

I nodded. "Should we look to see if there is one tonight?" I suggested as I held myself up with the back of a chair.

"No need," he said finally turning to look at me. "There is a huge Liga One match up tonight in town. Didn't you know?"

"No," I said quite honestly. Now, I remembered that I had heard a conversation about soccer in my hazy sleep and wondered what it had meant.

"Dinamo Bucharesti is playing Rapid Bucharesti, but it's

sold out," Hawkes informed me.

"Maybe Gray can get us tickets."

Hawkes shrugged his shoulders. "It's worth a shot, but he is American, so he probably won't be able to get any either."

"I'll call him." I stepped out onto the balcony with my cell phone so as not to disturb Hawkes.

Gray answered right away and seemed happy to hear from me. We chatted briefly before I awkwardly asked him for the favor. He told me that he wished he could, but he had already tried for some of his Romanian staff members. He had been unsuccessful. I thanked him anyway and we made tentative plans to hook up the next weekend.

"Any luck?" Hawkes asked as soon as I re-entered the apartment.

"No," I admitted glumly.

Go anyway . . .

This time the voice in my head was more like a thought and seemed to be directed at me.

Go to the stadium . . .

This was the strangest sensation in the world. Was I thinking these things or were they being placed there? And if they were, by whom? And why?

"We're still going," I told Hawkes.

CHAPTER THIRTEEN

Part of a text string between Sutton and his boys an hour later:

So, what happened?
I brought home this stud last night and he fucked my brains out
But when he woke up in the morning, he was different.
Aren't they all? LOL
No, not that way. He was physically different.
Not the same man.
How?
Shorter, less hairy, thinner, less muscled . . .
Maybe it was a different guy . . .
No, same face, same eyes, same voice
Were you drunk?
Not that much! LOL
I know it sounds crazy, but he knew it was going to happen.
And you know that buzzing noise in my head? It's gone now.
Completely?
Don't tell anyone but it's been replaced by thoughts or voices.
WTF?
I know . . . do you think I'm losing my mind?

Hawkes tried to talk me out of going to the stadium without tickets, but I was not to be deterred. I knew that he thought a soccer game was an unsafe venue for me and the thought of a rowdy, drunken group of soccer fans made me very nervous, but the voices in my head were driving me.

"Let's go grab something to eat and then we can go to the National Arena," I told him. "Wear something dressy — and red and white."

"Why?" he asked.

"I'm not sure. Just a feeling."

Minutes later I was dressed and ready to go. Hawkes looked good in a red and white striped button-down shirt and khakis. I had chosen to wear a red knit shirt with white carpenter pants. We looked like we were going to the carnival, but I was sure that we were going to fit right in at the stadium.

The normally grumpy doorman in the lobby suddenly smiled when he saw us exit the elevator. "You got tickets for the game?"

"Not really," I said. "But we are going to try."

The doorman laughed. "Good luck with that. Here, you'll need these." He handed me two stickers that were red and white shields. Inside the shields were two red wolf heads. He pulled back his suit jacket to show that he was wearing a soccer jersey of Dinamo.

I stuck one of the stickers on my chest and the other on Hawkes'. We took a taxi to the stadium but could only get within two blocks. Hawkes and I walked the rest of the way, enjoying the reverie of the crowd. All the bars and restaurants around the stadium were packed with fans, a lot of them dressed just like us.

The voices in my head were chatting a lot, but there were too many distractions for me to concentrate on what they were saying to each other. And now, I was pretty sure there were multiple voices. The smells from the crowd of NOMARs were already threatening to overwhelm my senses. The crowds were walking towards the main gates, but I pulled Hawkes to the right side.

"Over here," I said.

There was an entrance, small and unobtrusive further down the stadium wall. Two security guards were posted at the door. I walked confidently up to them while Hawkes hesitated.

I stood in front of the guards, not having a plan in my head for what I was going to say. "I'm Milos Saranac's brother and he told me to report here," I said suddenly surprising myself. I had spoken Romanian. Hawkes stared at me bug-eyed.

"Did he give you a security code?" one of the officers asked, also in Romanian which I suddenly understood perfectly.

I thought back to one of the conversations I had heard earlier in my head. "Six four seven two arsenal."

"Very good," the other officer said as he unlocked the door and pointed us to the elevators.

"What the fuck, Sutton?" Hawkes whispered.

"I'll tell you once we are in the suite."

"The suite?"

I pushed the call button for the elevator and said, "Yeah, suite number seven."

"How do you know that?"

"I just do," I whispered back as we stepped into the elevator. It took us right to the top floor of the stadium.

Hawkes and I exited the elevator and saw that the suites were numbered above the doors. Most of the doors were propped open and there were parties going on in each one of them. Many of the men looked at us with curiosity as we headed to number seven.

The door to our suite was closed and when we pushed it open, we saw the suite was empty of people while being well-stocked with beer, food, and plum brandy. We shut the door behind us.

Hawkes poured us each a shot of brandy and we clinked our glasses in salute to our brave escapade. We took seats in padded armchairs right up against the glass of the skybox.

"Now, tell me what's going on," Hawkes ordered me.

"Okay," I sighed. "That guy I took home last night."

"Boris?"

"Yes, him. Do you remember what he looked like?" I asked.

"Big ol' sucker—dark hair, dark beard, tall, muscular."

"Yes. Well, when I woke up, he wasn't the same."

Hawkes screwed up his face. "Wasn't the same? What do you mean?"

"I know this is going to sound crazy, but he had changed physically overnight."

"No way," he said immediately.

"I know. It sounds crazy, but he did and he knew that he had. He almost admitted it to me this morning."

"Okay, let's just say he did change. What does that have to do with this?"

"The buzzing in my head has stopped," I said bluntly.

He looked shocked. "Really? Since when?"

"Since this morning. It has been replaced."

"Replaced?"

"By voices," I said while nodding my head.

Hawkes didn't say anything, instead he just sat back in his chair looking at me like he didn't know whether I was pulling his leg or not.

"The voices don't seem to be talking to me but rather to each other. It's almost like I am listening into someone else's conversation."

"And they told you where to go tonight and what to say?" Hawkes asked.

"Not so much told me as they were talking and I overheard."

Hawkes still looked in disbelief at me. "And you speak Romanian now?"

"Apparently," I said with a chuckle. "I don't know how it works. Maybe I am going crazy."

"Are they talking now?"

"Yes."

"About what?"

"I haven't been able to concentrate. Shall I try now?"

"Yes. If someone is going to bust in here with us, I want to know about it in advance," Hawkes informed me, ever security minded. He nervously looked back at the closed door.

I swiveled my chair towards the field where the game was beginning and took another sip of my brandy. Now, that it was quiet, I could focus on the voices and I could hear seven distinct voices. And surprisingly, they were talking about the game.

"Stay in formation."

"Drive the ball to the left."

"Cross in front of the goal when I give the word."

"Now."

"Yes!"

The crowd went crazy as Dinamo scored a goal. The players all piled on the scorer on the sideline.

"They are talking about the game," I informed my bodyguard turned friend.

"Like they are watching it?"

I considered that for a moment and then answered, "It's like they are playing it."

"You're hearing the players down there?" he asked in shock.

"I think just the ones on Dinamo."

Hawkes picked up a pair of binoculars and trained them on the players on the pitch. I tried to hone in on the players themselves and suddenly felt my eyes adjust and then adjust again—refocusing each time until I could not only see the player, but I could see him up close. I could even see the sweat already running down his face.

I blinked my eyes, wondering how I was able to do this. However, instead of being frightened by it, I was thrilled. I moved to another player and then another as I looked at all of the players on the field in red and white. They were an incredibly handsome group of men, like a group of muscled, drop-dead gorgeous models who had formed a soccer club.

"Do you know which ones or can you hear all of them?" Hawkes asked without taking his eyes off of the pitch.

"It's not all of them."

I tried to focus on the voices while I was watching the players.

"*Watch the wing!*"

"*I'm coming up on your right, Dragomir.*"

"*Drive him towards us.*"

"*Intercept!*"

"*Running down the middle!*"

"*Swing it over to the left.*"

"*Hit me!*"

"*Scooooorrrrreeeee!*"

Dinamo scored again and led two goals to one. Half the crowd, the ones in red and white, went bonkers. I clapped and a slow smirk spread across my face.

Hawkes had put down the binoculars and was watching me. "What?"

"I think I can actually tell who is saying what," I said slowly.

"What did that fuck do to you?" he asked in a serious tone but then started to laugh to let me know that he was finding it all so hard to believe.

"I don't know," I admitted to him with a laugh of my own. "But it is so much better than the buzzing that was driving me out of my fucking mind."

"Is Boris one of the players?" Hawkes asked.

"No, but he's here," I said after taking a big whiff of the air in the skybox.

"You're like some kind of a freak," Hawkes said smiling at me.

"And getting freakier every day," I said, laughing. "Shall we eat?"

Hawkes nodded his agreement as the first half of the game ended.

CHAPTER FOURTEEN

Excerpt of the Dinamo's player biography page from the official program of the Bucharest Bowl:

Dragomir Iliac- Forward. Twenty-six-year-old from Cluj. Six-foot-one inch tall. One hundred seventy-nine pounds. Hobbies include wave-boarding, video games, and working out. "If I was not a professional football player, I would probably be a physical trainer."

Milos Saranac- Goalie. Twenty-nine-year-old from Bucharest. Six-foot-five-inches tall. Two hundred eight pounds. Hobbies include skiing, binge watching American TV shows, and speaking Italian. "If I was not a professional football player, I would probably be a professional basketball player."

Ivan Hpathaic- Defense. Twenty-one-year-old from Constanta. Six-foot-three-inches tall. One hundred ninety pounds. Hobbies include bowling, designing websites, and reading science fiction. "If I was not a professional football player, I would probably be an IT guy for some company."

Agair Mladonovic- Midfielder. Twenty-two-year-old from Bucharest. Six-foot-one-inch tall. One hundred eighty-seven pounds. Hobbies include playing on his hoverboard, cooking Italian food, and going to the movies. "If I was not a professional football player, I would probably be a chef in my own restaurant."

Alin Radonovic- Midfielder. Twenty-year-old from Mamula. Six-foot-two-inches tall. One hundred ninety-one pounds. Hobbies include playing his guitar, reading murder mysteries, and learning to play lacrosse. "If I was not a professional football player, I would probably be a detective, figuring out who done it."

"These men are big for soccer players," Hawkes said to me while he read the program. Neither one of us had gotten into the habit of calling it football yet.

"I know," I said. "They look like giants compared to the other team."

"And?" he asked, putting the program down.

"And what?"

"I know you noticed already . . ." he smirked.

I rolled my eyes and admitted, "Yes, they are an incredibly hot group of men."

"Just your type, I would say—bearded, muscled, tall, athletic."

"They do fall into the narrow guidelines that I have drawn for myself for sexual partners," I said sarcastically.

Hawkes laughed hard and repeated, "Narrow?"

"In my mind, Hawkes," I said settling back into the recliner and focusing on the game again. We were almost to the end of the game, but there was an injury timeout so the players were just standing on the field waiting.

For some reason, while I was waiting for play to resume, I consciously gave voice to my thoughts inside my head. *Hawkes is right, though. I would gladly get fucked by almost every one of these Dinamo players. They are by far the hottest men that I have seen since I've been in Romania.*

In one swift movement, seven players' heads snapped towards me in the skybox. Something told me that they had the same super focused vision I did, so I knew that they were looking right at me.

Slowly, I backed away from the glass and said, "We have to get out of here."

"What?" Hawkes asked with his mouth full of shrimp.

"We have to go, now." I turned and sprinted towards the door. Hawkes was right behind me.

We quickly walked towards the elevator which was fortunately waiting for us. Once inside it with the door closed, Hawkes asked, "What is going on?"

"They heard me," I stated simply. "Let me listen in." Hawkes was quiet so that I could do just that. I closed my eyes and concentrated.

"Who was that?"

"It was a wolf, but not from our pack."

"But how?"

"I don't know."

"Did you get a good look at him?"

"Not really. I was too shocked when I saw the mark."

"He's marked?"

"He can't be."

"But he definitely was."

"You heard what he said."

I flushed with embarrassment as I remembered what I had thought to myself. The elevator bell chimed that we had arrived at the ground level, so I hopped out and exited the stadium. The roars of the crowd covered our quick escape. Hawkes and I took a taxi back to our apartment.

"What happened?" my bodyguard asked me once we were alone again.

I told him about what I had thought and how a lot of the players that I had been watching reacted. He had a hard time wrapping his mind around the fact that we could indeed communicate telepathically but eventually got there. I told him what they had thought afterwards also.

"What do you think they meant when they called me a wolf?"

"No idea. Their mascot is two wolves, though."

"Do you think they are going to search for me?"

"Probably. If not to harm you, then to satisfy their curiosity."

"And by curiosity, you mean lust?"

"Yes," Hawkes said grimly.

"I was afraid of that. I'm exhausted listening in to other people's thoughts, so I'm going to bed."

"Want some company?" Hawkes asked with a raised eyebrow.

"Not tonight, Hawkes. I need to think through some stuff and your raging boner never lets me have time to think. Tomorrow, maybe."

He laughed and waved to me as he headed to his room. I had a lot to think about, but I was terrified to think so I didn't know what I was going to do.

Nine hours later, I woke from a fitful slumber having absolutely no answers to any of my questions. I didn't know what I wanted to do or how I was going to control my thoughts. What I did know was that I was starving.

I showered quickly and got ready. Hawkes was ready and waiting for me in the living room of our apartment. "Hungry?" I asked him.

"Yes."

"Let's go out."

"Do you think that is wise with what happened last night?"

"I'm not sure," I admitted. "But, one thing is for sure, I am not going to hide in this apartment all day, every day."

"Good on you," Hawkes said, obviously agreeing with me.

Hawkes and I walked to a local restaurant in Old Town and took a seat at a table nearer to the inside than the sidewalk. I was just starting to relax when I saw him.

One of the footballers from the game last night walked right in front of the restaurant. He stopped to talk to the host for a second before scanning the crowd. I kept my face hidden behind the over-sized menu while Hawkes described the action to me.

The professional soccer star eventually moved on and I was able to lower the menu. The host came right over to our table and said, "I told him that I hadn't seen you."

"Thanks," I told him with real gratitude.

"I don't care who he is, you have a right to your privacy," the restaurant host continued.

"Thank you so much. May I ask what he asked you?"

"He asked if I had seen a marked American in this section of town. I said that I had not. He gave me this to use if I do see you." He put a solid red card down on our table.

The card only had a single word on it and a cell phone number in white. The word on the card was *Copoi*. I looked up at the host with a curious look on my face.

"It means Hounds," he translated for me. I hadn't needed him to since I now read Romanian, but it kept me from having to explain my new-found powers.

"Ever heard of it before?"

"No."

"Thanks for your help," I told him.

"Yeah, no problem." The host was awkwardly waiting on something and I had a feeling I knew just what it was.

"You want a reward, do you?" I put him out of his misery. He was pretty good looking—slightly shorter than me but with a thick broad chest that I was pretty sure I was going to like. He was probably in his thirties, bald with a dark blond full beard.

He smiled, lighting up his face. "That would be nice, but you don't have to."

"What's your name?"

"Bill."

"Hi, Bill. I'm Sutton. You can take me to dinner tonight and we'll see."

"Yes? Holy shit!"

I chuckled. "Now go away and let me eat with my

friend."

"Yes, sir!" he said quickly as he left for the host stand.

"See, Hawkes," I said, turning to my bodyguard. "That NOMAR has already surrendered his control to me. He's going to be no fun at all." I reconsidered for a moment. "Well, he'll be a little fun."

For the rest of the afternoon, I laid low until it was time for the dinner with Bill. He wanted to take me to some new Indian place that he had heard of across the river. Bill and I had just exited the taxi when I saw one of the soccer players emerge from the restaurant.

I quickly turned around so that he couldn't see me. Bill turned around and followed where I was looking before I stopped. I heard his sharp intake of breath as he obviously saw the player. To his credit, Bill didn't say anything, but just stood between me and the athlete until he got into a car and left.

While at dinner, I had to tell Bill why I was being stalked by the Romanian soccer players, but I made up a story involving a hot orgy that covered my lies. I excused myself to go to the restroom. It was empty and quiet, so I sat down on the john and put my head in my hands.

I concentrated on the voices that were muted in my head. Once the volume was turned up, the conversations flooded my subconscious like a wave breaking on the shore. It was hard to focus on any one voice at first, but I soon got the hang of it.

"Any luck guys?"

"None so far."

"He used to stay at a hotel in the political district, but he's gone from there now."

"Forwarding address?"

"None given."

"Why would he be in a hotel there? That's not where tourists go."

"Don't know. You want me to canvas the area tomorrow?"
"Yes."
"We have to find him."
"What if he is listening in on us right now?"
"Then you better hurry."

CHAPTER FIFTEEN

A section of a text string between Gray Carron and Sutton
Pike, May twenty-fifth:

Sutton, you okay?
Sure, Gray. What's up?
We just had an inquiry about you . . .
Oh, yeah?
Yes. Are you in trouble?
I don't think so, but you're sweet to worry about me.
Some of these people are not to be taken lightly, Sutton
I'm not sure they want to harm me, Gray
You better find out
Yes, sir!
Don't be flippant about this, Sutton
I worry about you
Thanks! I really do appreciate you looking out for me
Can I help you in any way?
*Not that I can think of, but I will let you know when if I need
you*
You better
Call you soon

I was finally picked up on a Friday night. I had taken all the
quiet hiding time that I could stand. I was horny as hell and
was hoping to waltz into the club, quickly pick out a hot
man to fuck, and then leave. It had gone exactly according to

plan until I left the club.

The man that I had connected with was Ianu, and he was a lumberjack—literally a lumberjack. He looked like one and he was one. He was visiting Bucharest from the Carpathian Mountains where he worked. I figured he was safe since he was on holiday and not from town.

I was wrong.

Ianu showed me to his truck, which was a large construction truck like the ones that were popular in the United States. Normally, I wouldn't have ridden with him, but I knew that Hawkes was trailing us and we were headed to my apartment, so I took the risk.

When Ianu missed the turn for the historic part of the city where I lived, I turned to him. "You know that my bodyguard is following us, don't you?"

"That brown-haired muscle-head?"

"That's him. Don't do anything stupid."

"He's being taken care of right now," the big lumberjack said softly.

"You're not going to hurt him, are you?" I asked in a panic.

"No. His way is going to be blocked just about now," Ianu said just as I saw a huge construction vehicle pull out right behind us and block the street.

"And what is your plan for me?" I asked, level-headed. I had been in too many sketchy situations where I had learned that the calmer I could stay, the better.

"I have big plans for you, just you wait and see," he grinned. His smile wasn't scary, but more lust-filled. And since I was going to fuck with him anyway . . .

"Should I be scared?" I asked with a smirk.

"Not if you like cock," he smirked back.

"I do like that," I said dreamily. Getting serious again, I asked, "So, I'm not going to be in danger?"

"You will survive."

"Good to know. You're not even a lumberjack, are you?"

"Lawyer."

"Fuck me," I said with chagrin as I realized the extent of the deception. He looked nothing like a lawyer with his six-foot-five-inch frame and linebacker body. His long black beard reminded me more of Duck Dynasty than LA Law. His blue eyes sparkled at me in his handsome face.

"That's the plan."

I was still trying to put the puzzle pieces together since I was pretty much powerless in this situation. "Were you in that bar looking for me?"

"No. Just got lucky, I guess."

"Where are we going?"

"We're here," Ianu stated.

We had pulled up to a warehouse on the outskirts of town. It didn't look like a place that I would want to be.

"Can I send a text to Hawkes to let him know that I am not in any physical danger?"

"If you must. You are not a hostage . . . yet." The fake lumberjack pulled into a parking lot and turned the truck off. "Don't tell him where you are or even describe the place," he growled.

I sent the text while Ianu watched me. When I was done, my captor held his big hand out and I placed my cell phone into it.

"Get out," he ordered.

I did what he wanted and followed him to a door in the side of the warehouse. Instead of a lock, the door had a scanner beside it. I expected Ianu to place his palm or eye on the smooth glass plate of the scanner, instead he opened his mouth wide and held it still.

What the hell am I involved with? Who has a dental scanner at their warehouse?

The door opened and Ianu held it for me. I tentatively

stepped inside and lights automatically blazed on. It was an innocent looking reception room.

"Strip," he ordered.

I wasn't sure I wanted to get naked just yet without knowing what was going to happen. I stood still.

"Strip," Ianu growled at me.

I slowly started to take off my clothes. Ianu stood with his giant arms crossed across his chest watching me. I took my time and folded my clothes into a pile on a nearby chair.

Once I was completely naked, the devious lawyer motioned with his finger for me to spin around. I did.

"Very nice," he said with a sharp intake of breath.

I bowed since I didn't know what else to do.

"Follow me." He turned towards the inside door. This time the scanner was for his hand.

The door popped open and Ianu stepped inside. The lights came on and I saw a whole wall of warehouse shelving containing crates. There were dollies parked on the side and a series of pulleys and cranes on the ceiling.

Ianu walked up to one of the crates and opened its door. That's when I saw that these things on the shelves were not crates, but cages. They were not the handcrafted, expensive cages that were made by The Service like the one that I was delivered to my Master inside. My cage had been a thing of beauty—smooth bamboo floors and ceiling with gleaming bars of steel. I could see that these were crudely made compared to the ones I knew.

"Get in," Ianu said firmly.

"Oh, hell no," I said equally as firmly.

"Get in." He was back to growling again.

I was defiant and thought that I would have a better chance of getting out of this situation if I had some assurances first. But in this case, I wasn't sure how to demand them. I needed to use my leverage. I wasn't even sure if Ianu was part of the group that was looking for me or not, but I had a hunch that he was. I got an idea and decided that it was worth a shot.

In all of the chatter in my head over the past few weeks, one thing I had noticed was that there was no voice of authority or command. It seemed odd to me that there would not be one person in charge and I began to wonder if there was someone who was just purposely staying quiet amongst all the noise. That person was who I needed to appeal to.

I bowed my head and put my hands on either side of my temples. I spoke the words aloud inside my head as I thought them.

"I will not be caged like the others of my kind. I have special skills that I possess beyond others. I call to you, the one known as Alpha. I seek an audience with you."

I heard Ianu's sharp intake of breath and his face suddenly went white. "You are a werewolf?" he asked quickly.

I almost laughed in his face, "No. Are you?"

"Yes," came the simple answer.

Before Ianu could ask another question, a deep booming voice appeared in my head and I knew instantly that it was the alpha. Something about his voice affected me immediately. His voice was as smooth as still water but had a quiet power like a coiled snake ready to strike. I was drawn to it and scared of it at the same time. My cock rose majestically towards the ceiling.

"Ianu, shut your fucking mouth."

"Yes, sir."

"Bring the brash one to me."

"Yes, sir."

"And Ianu . . ."

"Yes, sir?"

"Bring him in the cage."

The beefy lawyer's eyes focused on me, and he growled again from somewhere deep inside his chest. He leveled his arm and pointed with one big finger towards the cage that stood open and ready.

I bowed to him and headed towards the open door. I climbed into the cage and held onto the rough bars as he slammed the door shut and locked it with a padlock.

"That should keep you safe."

"From you, the werewolf, Ianu?" I challenged him. He had to be bullshitting me, but he had definitely been serious when he had asked me if I was one.

"Yes."

"And the cage will protect you from me also," I said with a confidence that I didn't quite feel.

Ianu chuckled. "I'm not the one you have to worry about."

"What does that mean?" I challenged him.

"You are getting ready to go before the alpha."

"Yeah, so?" I asked, cautiously.

He smiled a lopsided grin at me through the bars of the cage. "Most people don't return from an audience with the alpha."

I felt my stomach lurch into my throat. "What does he do?"

"You'll see," he said mysteriously as he slid a dolly under my cage and jacked it up before wheeling me towards the loading dock ramp.

CHAPTER SIXTEEN

A letter found crammed between the rough floorboards of the cage that Sutton was being carried in on his way to meet the alpha:

To whoever is in this cage now,

My name is Petor and I was once in your place. I am a student at the University of Transylvania. One day one of my professors caught me cheating on my exams. He called me to his office and showed me evidence he had collected where I had been cheating for years. There was no way that I could deny it, so I admitted it.

He gave me a drink and the next thing I knew I was in a warehouse. My professor told me that he was going to wash away my sins. He made me strip and he painted a vibrant blue mark on the side of my face. And then he locked me in this cage.

It doesn't take a rocket scientist to know how I am going to pay for my crimes. I hope that it doesn't hurt too much, and I fear that you are headed for the same fate as me, my friend.

Good luck.

The note that I had found did little to ease my mind or answer any questions for me. I was still amazed that I could read Romanian and wasn't quite used to it yet. The note must have been hastily scribbled, probably in the dark, and read in the same way, so it had taken me a while to figure it all out. I didn't feel that I was in as bad a predicament as the NOMAR who had been in the cage and had written the note — at least I would enjoy it to a degree.

Carefully folding the note back into its small tube-shape, I placed it back between the floorboards where I had found it. "For the next guy," I said, to no one in particular.

I was currently riding in the back of a delivery van on my way to being delivered to the alpha. I supposed that Ianu, the lawyer who claimed to have been a lumberjack in order to pick me up, was driving but I did not know that for certain. The van did have windows and the cage did not have a heavy curtain around it like the ones from The Service did, so I was able to see a little bit. We were headed out of town.

The van took a road leading into the mountains. I was aware that this road was west of the normal route taken by tourists. I had already explored the mountains to the north and seen all of the tourist attractions, so this section of the Carpathians was new to me. It looked like the rest of the countryside, but it concerned me that it was off the beaten path.

We climbed and climbed up into the mountains, finally coming to an impressive stone wall that seemed to go on for miles. I wondered what the wall was surrounding. The movement of the van slowed and then stopped at a tremendously large gate set into the high rock walls of the border. The gate looked very sturdy like it was made of iron. I looked hard into the dark of the forest behind the wall but could see nothing but blackness.

Ianu parked the van and got out of it. I could barely see him through the side window, but I saw that he was using multiple body parts again to gain entrance. But the last security measure came crashing through the silence of the back of the van like a sudden clap of thunder.

"Do you have him, Ianu?"

"Yes, sir."

"Can you hear me, little one who thinks he is so special?"

His voice seemed to penetrate my body right to my soul.

It reverberated in my nut sack and caused all the hair on my body to stand at attention. Cold chills formed on my arms.

"Yes, sir."

Why was I being so deferential to him? I didn't know him from Adam, but it just seemed to come naturally.

"Once you enter our house, you will no longer have control. There will be no demands."

Oh, shit. What am I getting myself into? Not like I really had a choice to start with because I had already been captured, but I had made demands to have an audience with the alpha.

"Do you understand?"

"Yes, sir."

"Bring him in, Ianu."

The alpha's voice disappeared from my thoughts just like it had come, leaving me feeling empty and alone. My cock was rock hard again and I shivered from the effect that he had on my body. This man seemed to have some kind of power over me that I couldn't explain and I hadn't even met him yet.

Ianu got back into the van and drove us forward. I watched the heavy iron gates close behind us out of the back window. The driveway was a long winding path through dense forest. It was obvious that the grounds on this estate were pristine forest, undisturbed by man. The scope of the property must be amazing based on the limited information I had.

The night was dark as fuck. I didn't know how the fake lumberjack was even finding his way, but he drove smoothly without even a moment of hesitation. Suddenly, I saw a glimmer of light in the darkness—small and warm like a campfire. The flame got brighter and bigger as we drove further into the woods. The flames turned out to be the blazing lights of a house, and it was a huge house.

I watched through the metal bars in amazement as the

house came into view. It was a fucking mansion done in the Gothic style. Three floors of windows shone light into the dark night, although we were so far into the forest that I doubted any could be seen. The front drive was lined with some of the most expensive sports cars and luxury vehicles that I had ever seen—Mercedes, Jaguars, Porsches, Lamborghinis, Morgans, and Maseratis.

The house, if you could call something so large that, was made of stone and the most beautiful dark wood that I had ever seen. The very small front drive was beautifully landscaped and the house looked inviting as hell. I couldn't see any signs of life.

Ianu stopped the van right at the front door. He exited the vehicle and opened the back doors. Suddenly, he was joined by two others. The two new men were hot as hell and dressed to the nines. They had a weird looking contraption with them that grasped the bars of my cage and lifted me out of the back of the van. One of them was working a remote that was controlling the robot holding me. It looked like the machine would be top-heavy, especially after it picked me up, but I felt very secure even as the treads of the robot travelled over asphalt and climbed stairs.

The huge front door opened into a lavishly decorated foyer with a wide marble staircase leading to the second floor. There was a gigantic urn filled with fresh flowers right in the middle of the room. We turned left towards a set of double doors into what I had to assume was a huge ballroom based on the noise. I could smell the sex way before I could see it. There was a strong smell of testosterone, cum, and sweat coming from the house. My stomach growled as I also smelled food. I couldn't tell how many men were in the house based on their smells, but I knew there were at least ten men here whose smell I would like to smell more of.

Once in the ballroom, I saw gorgeous men everywhere.

The room was lit with what seemed like a thousand candles. All of the men were in tuxedos, some in various stages of undress. I was impressed by the endowment of the men whose pants were off and found it hard to focus on anything else. My eyes drank in the landscape of lurid sex acts happening all around me on every possible surface. I felt my face heat up as I recognized some of the football players from the game the other week.

Against the far wall was a make-shift stage holding ten cages just like mine. Most of them were open and their occupants bent over the nearest couch or on top of a nearby coffee table. I watched with fascination as one NOMAR blew a load down one of the fake marked man's throat and then returned him to one of the cages to wait for the next man.

My head exploded with sound as I was carried into the room. This was not the alpha's voice, booming and commanding. These were the thoughts of the beautiful men around me.

"Is this the one?"

"The one from the football game."

"He's here."

"He's the lone wolf that we have been looking for?"

"The American."

"He's here."

"The marked man that can hear our thoughts."

"How can he hear us when he is not a member of our pack?"

"His mark is real?"

"How can he be marked and a wolf?"

"What else can he do?"

"He's here."

"He is going to see the alpha."

"Oh, fuck."

I greeted each handsome NOMAR in my head as I was paraded past them. Most of them reached through the cage bars and touched my mark. I wasn't sure why they were doing this, but I let them. Each of us got a good whiff of the other's scent when this happened.

Even the men that were fucking the shit out of some poor guy who probably deserved it, stopped in mid-thrust to ex-am me as I came by. One marked man was close enough for me to touch, so I reached out and touched his mark like the others were doing to me.

Drawing my fingers back into my cage, I saw that there was blue on them and I immediately remembered the letter that I had found in my cage. I came to the realization that all of these men getting railed out were probably NOMARs in disguise.

As Ianu and I moved further into the ballroom, I saw a lavish display of food set up buffet style. Next to the food was a fully furnished bar that was being manned by a marked man. His crime must have been especially terrible to have to work while he was getting his punishment. I had never seen a group of men so handsome assembled in one place in my whole life. It didn't hurt that they were all my type either — tall, muscular, handsome, thick, bearded, mas-culine, sexy, tatted, bad boys. I yearned to be out of this cage and right in the middle of all of this sex. For one of the first times in my life, I felt overwhelmed by my senses. My cock was painfully hard, my nostrils were full of man-musk, and my eyes were wide with the visions of mortal gods dominat-ing their own.

Ianu headed for the door as I met the last few men in tux-edos. The robot controlling my cage followed him. The rest of the house was quiet, but occasionally I saw a faux-marked man in a room being whipped or punished in some way by a handsome NOMAR.

I was wide-eyed as Ianu approached a heavy-looking set of ornately carved wooden doors. He knocked and was told to come inside. It was the alpha's voice, deep, husky, and commanding. The blood coursed through my veins and straight to my cock.

Ianu pushed open the heavy doors and stepped inside. Moving forward, I could see that we were in a long reception room although, I couldn't see what was at the end because of the fake lumberjack in front of me, but I desperately tried. The room smelled like sweat, sex, and something else.

The forward momentum of my cage stopped, and Ianu moved to the side of the narrow room. He now had the remote control guiding the robot that was holding my cage. He manipulated it so that I was lowered to the floor. I was still trying to figure out the smell in the room as my eyes blinked adjusting to the dim candlelight.

In front of me was a huge carved wooden chair made to resemble a throne. It was elevated on a dais consisting of three or four steps. Perched on top of the throne was a huge fucking man. And he was currently fucking a man.

Suddenly I realized what the smell was that had been filling my nostrils since I entered the room. The smell was so complex because it was a combination of two smells. However, there was nothing subtle about it. I could easily identify it over the smells of sex, sweat, and man in this room.

This man smelled like two of my favorite things—fresh pineapple and new tennis balls.

CHAPTER SEVENTEEN

A list of the men being punished by the Hounds on the same night on which I had an audience with the alpha:

Petre W: twenty, Bucharest, cyber crimes against the elderly
Octavian B: thirty-four, Bucharest, assault and battery
Anton A: twenty-five, Mamula, indecent exposure to school children
Ciprian D: thirty-nine, Constanta, identity theft
Decebal P: forty-four, Siegishora, grand theft auto
Emillan F: nineteen, Iasi, home invasion
Matei M: twenty-one, Brasov, driving while impaired
Nicu O: thirty, Brasov, drug trafficking
Santu R: twenty-two, Brasov, running a meth lab
Iancu G: twenty-seven, Sinaia, home arson
Teodor I: thirty-two, Sibu, insurance fraud
Adrian D: thirty-four, Cluj-Napoca, public intoxication
Stefan Z: twenty-eight, Timisoara, public intoxication
Benjamin P: twenty-three, Craiova, hate crimes
Lucian L: forty, Galati, credit card fraud
Gavril W: forty-five, Ploiesti, assault and battery

The alpha wolf took one hard look at Ianu and then at me in the cage.

Looking back at him, I watched as the big man stopped what he was doing, pulled on the little man's neck, and sat him on the dais to the side of his chair.

My breath caught in my throat. I didn't know if the big man had done it for my benefit or not, but it was an amazing show of strength. This man's muscles were amazing but nothing was as terrifying as the size of his cock.

"Return to your cage," the alpha commanded the little man. His voice was even more amazing now that I was in his presence.

Without even a word, the fake-marked man scrambled to his feet and took off out the doors. The quiet receiving room reverberated with the closing of the heavy wooden door after his departure. I watched the big man closely as the silence hung in the air between us.

The alpha stood up and my eyes widened so much that they hurt. He was huge but with an absolutely beautiful body. His face was sexy as hell, but the thing I noticed after his smell was his eyes. They were ice blue and seemed to penetrate into the darkest recesses of my soul when he gazed at me.

The alpha stepped down from the dais. He was completely naked and his over-sized cock swung between his legs like a cricket bat—thick and long. Strangely, it had several dark lines circumnavigating the shaft. The alpha had brown hair that was brushed over his head with a European part cut high into his hairline. The sides of his head were shaved tight to his skull. The alpha was very handsome with a full beard that matched his hair.

The man who smelled like my favorite things had a thick chest, muscled like a Roman centurion in his armor. He had tattoos on both pectoral muscles that carried down onto each bicep. A washboard stomach was covered in brown hair that made a trail down to his pubic hair.

The alpha's hairy thighs were some of the largest on a normal human that I had ever seen. He looked like he might have been a bodybuilder, but his movement was so smooth and easy that I instantly knew he couldn't be. His walk was effortless but predatory at the same time. It very much reminded me of a wolf.

He walked straight to Ianu, grabbed each of his shoulders, and kissed him on both cheeks. "You have done well, Ianu."

"Thank you, Alpha."

They were talking in Romanian, and I assumed they realized that I could understand them.

"You will be rewarded in a little while," the alpha told him.

"Thank you, sir," he said with genuine emotion.

"Go get something to eat and bring something back for your captive," the alpha said without even turning to look at me.

Ianu hesitated and shot a quick glance at me. "What do you think he would like to eat, sir?"

The alpha was not happy when he spoke next. He raised his voice and loudly snapped, "Who gives a fuck what he would like, Ianu? He will eat what you bring him or he will go without. Do you understand?"

"Yes, sir. Sorry, sir."

"Go," he ordered.

Ianu left the hall quickly and then there was just the two of us. The alpha approached my cage and removed the lock from the door. He looked even bigger up close, especially his cock. Being this close to him, I could see that the alpha had dark lines tattooed onto the shaft of his cock. There were at least three of them that I could see.

The alpha did not even look into my cage while he was near me. His smell was so strong that it made me lightheaded. I did notice that since I had entered the room, the noise and voices in my head had ceased. He headed back to his chair.

"Come out of your cage, special one," he said flippantly to me as he climbed the steps to his seat. His feet were on full display right in front of my eyes and my balls were literally on fire as I stared at them. The alpha was speaking English now, and his delivery of it was excellent. He was a very unique man.

I pushed the door open and gingerly stepped out of the cage before straightening up.

"Hmph," the alpha commented as I stood. "Come here," he ordered, pointing with a finger to the hardwood floor in front of his chair.

I walked slowly towards him, carefully like I was approaching a lion.

"Kneel," he commanded.

I did, but I also decided to test him. "Yes, sir."

He growled, "Don't speak unless I ask you a question, brash one. If you do it again, you will be punished."

Wow. This man has potential. I nodded that I understood.

He placed his hand on his hairy chin and scratched it. When the alpha finally spoke to me, his booming voice left no room for disobedience. "Why should I care what you want?"

I swallowed hard and blurted out, "Because I am unlike any marked man that you have encountered before."

"You will address me with respect, little one, or I will turn you over my knee right now," he said firmly.

Is he serious? Will he really make me lay across his legs while he spanks me? The thought excited me and terrified me at the same time. "Sorry, sir," I spat out quickly.

"And what makes you so special?" he challenged.

I was ready for this question. "I'm not sure, but I can hear you and your men, sir."

"Yeah, I don't know how you are doing that, but I will find out," he said with such confidence that there was no question in my mind that he would. "What else?"

"I'm not sure, but I think you and your men use smell the same way I do," I offered up to him, "sir," I quickly added.

"And in what way is that?" He had not smiled since I had been in the same room with him. And he was not smiling now.

"For location and identification, sir," I answered.

"Really?"

I could have sworn that I saw a very brief shadow of shock cross the alpha's handsome face.

"Are you a werewolf?" he abruptly asked. There was not a hint of humor or sarcasm on the alpha's face.

I chuckled and started to say, "You're the second . . ."

"Answer me!" he roared as he stood.

"No, sir," I said, quickly.

"Then you are something else," he said calmly as he sat back down. "Tell me."

"I don't know. I didn't even know that werewolves were real and kinda still don't, sir," I stammered.

"They are."

"How do you know, sir?"

He grinned for the first time, but it was not a pleasant smile. It was predatory and powerful. "Because you are speaking to one right now."

My first instinct was to laugh out loud, but my second one was to piss myself. I swallowed hard, trying to decide what to say. "Sir, can't you just tell if I'm one?" I finally asked.

"Your smell is not entirely lycan," he said with his serious face again.

I was surprised by this news. "You mean I smell somewhat like a werewolf, sir?"

"Yes," he said, standing up once again. The alpha slowly stepped down the steps towards me. I got a great view of his naked feet as he walked around my kneeling body. I could also feel the heat waves coming off his skin. "And then again, there has never been a marked wolf before, so maybe your smell is just different from ours."

The alpha stopped in front of me. I couldn't bring myself to look up at him.

"Look at me!" he snapped.

I looked up into his handsome face, getting drawn into his icy blue gaze like a moth to a spotlight.

The alpha reached down and touched my mark. He rubbed it, but it did not come off. His hand was hot on my skin. The heat pouring off his naked body and the smell of him was so strong that I thought I would pass out being this close to him.

"You are hot," he remarked.

"Thank you, sir," I said flippantly.

"Your temperature, asshole." The alpha snorted.

"Is that significant?" I asked. He glared at me and I quickly added his term of respect.

He ordered me, "Feel mine."

I reached out and touched his broad chest. I wanted to touch his huge cock that was right in front of my face, but I didn't have the courage. His skin was hot to my touch.

"You're hot also, sir," I stated in wonder.

"Thank you," he said, just as flippantly as I had.

I rolled my eyes.

The alpha drew in a sharp intake of breath before growling, "If you belonged to me, I would blacken those eyes for rolling them at me."

"Lucky that I'm not, then, sir," I said almost in a whisper.

"We shall see about that. Wolves run hot."

This man's words had the ability to set my loins on fire. The very thought that this god-in-human-form might want to be my Master turned me on so much that I felt amazing. "I am not a werewolf," I said in exasperation. "But I do have some questions for you, if you don't mind answering them for me, sir."

The alpha growled from deep inside his big chest. "I should just bite you and then this foolishness will be over." Just to add another layer of distraction to what he was saying, my new infatuation lifted one leg and swung it over the heavy wooden arm of his chair. His crotch was now fully exposed to me.

"Why would that change anything?" I asked in horror forgetting his term of respect.

"Approach," he growled.

Fuck! He's really going to do this! I stood and slowly walked up the steps to his chair. He lowered his leg so that his thighs made a big table. Motioning to me to lie over them, he smirked hard at me.

I took a deep breath, decided to just go for it, and prostrated myself across his legs. In my mind, I didn't think he would really do it. The first whack of his open hand on my exposed ass drove that thought right out of my mind.

The man who thought he was a werewolf hit me with such force that I was driven forward. Tears appeared in my eyes instantly. My ass stung from the hit and the second whack was even harder. It hurt worse this time since my ass was already stinging. Even his throbbing cock against my stomach couldn't take my mind off the pain.

"I will not be toyed with, little one. Tell me that you know this now."

"Yes, sir."

"Good. Now, return to your place on your knees in front of me," he commanded.

I did, grimacing when my ass cheeks touched the heels of my feet as I knelt. He didn't apologize for spanking me or comment on my tears. At first, that slight made me angry, but then I realized that a true Master would not apologize or concern himself with these trivial matters.

"In answer to your question, my Servant, if I bite you, I would have the answers to all of my questions and you would be forced to obey me!"

"You don't know me very well, sir," I said to him. Seeing his icy stare, I turned serious and asked, "Not that I don't want you to bite me, sir, but why would that give you answers?"

"If you are bitten by the wolf, you will become a werewolf and I will know your thoughts. I will be able to taste the answers in your blood."

"Oh." I still wasn't sure that these people were who they claimed to be, but I had to admire their commitment to the story.

Before I could ask another question, the door opened and Ianu backed in with two plates of food. He placed them on the top of my cage.

"Eat, Ianu," the alpha ordered. He started walking towards the door. "I have business to take care of, but when I get back, I want to see you fuck the shit out of our special friend here."

Chapter Eighteen

Part of a report by Stephen Hawkes on assignment in Bucharest, Romania filed with his employer on June eighth:

On the night of June seventh, my client, Sutton Pike, was abducted.

I have filed a missing person report with the local authorities this morning.

Below is a recounting of the events of that night.

I escorted Sutton Pike to a sports bar called the Bucha-Relax located on Grindavain Street at approximately nine o'clock p.m. The bar was crowded, but Sutton met a lumberjack from the mountains. His name, according to his identification was Ianu Mirce.

After talking for over an hour, Sutton informed me that he was going to take him home. Sutton planned to ride with Ianu in his truck with me following. He was directed to go back to our apartment. Ianu was last seen driving a white Chevrolet two thousand fifteen Silverado fifteen hundred HD with a Romanian license plate reading RT 13 RAV.

I followed the truck until Ianu missed the turn for our apartment. I sped up and tried to intercept but was cut off by a construction truck at the intersection of Hais and Leva Streets. By the time the vehicle moved, the truck was gone.

I suspect that the driver of the construction vehicle is in on the abduction, but I cannot find any link between him and Ianu. The Chevy truck has been traced to a business that rents vehicles to its members. They are free to pick any vehicle without paperwork. The authorities have asked for their membership list.

I ate cautiously due to my stomach being in knots. I was still picking at my food when the alpha came back into the room. His stride was effortless and purposeful, even though he was completely naked. This man was sexy as hell.

"Enough. Time to fuck," the big man growled at me as he walked by, leaving a trail of his smell in his wake, but not even looking in my direction.

What was it about this man that excited me so much? He had an effect on me that no man had really had before. It had to be lust. I wanted him badly. I wanted that big cock inside me, stretching me out, making me whine and moan beneath him.

The alpha wolf walked behind his chair and came back with a rectangle of foam covered in cloth. He threw that down in front of his chair and climbed the dais. I couldn't help but notice that he sat in his chair with one leg cocked over one of the arms, giving me full visual access to his crotch. His over-sized fingers lightly ran up and down the bottom vein of his big shaft, making my own dick hard as a rock.

Ianu started to undress while I moved to the foam bedding in front of the alpha. I kneeled and waited for him with my back to the alpha. I was cognizant that my ass was pointed at the alpha and that his eyes were burning a hole into the back of me.

The lawyer-turned-lumberjack did not disappoint me once he was naked. Ianu had a fabulous body—muscular, well-developed, thick, and hairy. His cock was pretty long and thick with veins that ran all along the shaft. He walked over to me and fed it into my hungry hole. I was surprised that his cock was throwing off so much heat, since the room was a little chilly.

I sucked him hard with long drawing pulls that hollowed out my cheeks. Ianu held my head as I worked him over. I was very aware that I was auditioning for the alpha as much as I was trying to please the man whose cock was currently filling my mouth. I continued to blow him until he was hard as a steel beam.

"Fuck him now, Ianu," the alpha demanded.

"Yes, Alpha," Ianu said as he pulled his big dong out of my wet mouth.

I laid down on my back and pulled my legs up to my chest. Ianu stepped into the saddle and his soft cock head was soon pressing against my puckered hole. With nothing but my saliva on his cock as lube, Ianu shoved his laphog home.

I moaned shamelessly as Ianu rammed his full length into my ass. His cock felt really good as it stretched out my anal ring. When he leaned over me holding himself up with his big arms and started pumping his dick back and forth inside me, I felt my eyes roll back in my head. His hot cock was heating up my guts from the inside.

"Fuck me," I moaned.

"You are so fucking tight," Ianu groaned between clenched teeth.

"Faster," the alpha ordered. "Test him."

Why isn't the big alpha testing me himself? At this point, I couldn't really think about it because Ianu was giving me the fucking that I needed.

Ianu pulled my left leg to his right side and then lay down behind me. Lifting my leg up and behind his top leg, he scooched closer to me and then began to fucking rock me with that big cock again.

We were both sweating like crazy as Ianu hunched into my sweet ass over and over. The strain eventually proved too much, and he lost his shit and filled my sore ass up with his sweet cream. Ianu had grunted loudly as he filled me with his seed. Now, he sighed in complete satisfaction as the tension in his body left him and he relaxed behind me.

"Again," the alpha said with such a demanding voice that I knew there would be no resistance on my part.

Ianu pulled his cock out of me, and I flipped around to suck him up hard again. I was on all fours on the mat.

"Just like that, Ianu," the alpha demanded. "Show him how doggy-style should be done."

Ianu got hard quickly and was soon feeding his big cock back into my puckered hole. His last load of cum eased the way this time, but that was the easiest thing about this fuck. Ianu put on a show for the alpha—fucking me so hard and aggressively that I thought my asshole was going to catch fire from the friction of the fuck and from the heat his body was throwing off.

I wanted to grab my prick and stroke it while Ianu was fucking me so hard, but I could just barely hold myself up as it was. My arms were shaky, and Ianu was working my body back and forth like an oil derrick.

Raising my face up to the alpha's eyes, I opened my mouth and howled. No sound escaped my mouth since I had only thought it. Instantly, both the alpha and Ianu opened their mouths wide and repeated my howl. I got a flash of an image of every werewolf in the ballroom doing the same thing.

I felt myself on the edge of my climax and then I realized that I was going to cum without even touching myself. Quickly wondering if the howl had been the final impetus that I had needed to reach my orgasm, I dismissed the thought as I pumped hot cum onto the mat underneath me.

The fake lumberjack used my hips to slam into his with each thrust. He was able to go a lot longer this time, since he had already cum once. My ass muscles constricted due to my orgasm, and Ianu was soon blowing his load deep inside me and completely collapsing on top of my back in exhaustion. My arms were so shaky that I wasn't sure that I could hold him up.

"Very good, Ianu. I am proud of you," the alpha told his pack member. He had stood up from his chair and walked down to us. He helped Ianu stand while I opportunistically studied his wide masculine feet. They were beautiful and I couldn't wait until I could get my lips on them.

"You have done well and I will promote you to Game Warden at the next council meeting."

Ianu's face went ashen white suddenly. "Alpha?" he asked in disbelief.

"You have earned it tonight, Ianu. This one is actually as special as he claims to be, and you are the one who has brought him to us, so you deserve the reward."

"Thank you, Alpha," Ianu said with a slight bow.

"Now, leave us. I have much to discuss with the special one."

"Yes, sir."

After that rough fucking, there was no way I could sit down, so I kneeled on the pad in front of the alpha's chair and made sure that my ass did not touch my legs as I settled in. My heart was racing and my breathing was faster than it should have been.

Ianu left the hall and the alpha walked up to where I was kneeling with my head bowed. Standing in front of me, his smell was just as intoxicating to me as the sight of his strong masculine feet which were almost more than I could take.

"What shall I do with you, little one?"

"*Fuck me . . .*"

"Well, that is definitely going to happen, little one, but the question is what to do with you. Look at me," he commanded. "You are too important to let go and too different to include." The alpha sat down on the steps in front of me and rubbed his bearded face. His icy blue eyes burned a hole into my soul.

I tried hard to think of a solution that would make both of us happy, but the closeness of his body and the stare of his eyes kept me distracted just enough to not be able to concentrate.

"I will just bite you and see what happens," he finally informed me.

"Okay, let's skip the biting for now and try to forge something else, sir," I responded quickly.

"What then is your proposal?" he asked in exasperation.

Now I had to scramble to think of something else. "Well, sir, it seems to me that you want me to be obedient and to figure out what I am exactly. And I want to submit to you and figure out what is going on with me. I have a lot of questions."

"Yes, so?"

"How about I spend a day or two as your Servant? I will be completely obedient to you . . . well, as much as I can be. You will answer my questions and I will answer yours. You will have time to figure out what I am and what you may want to do with me. If that is agreeable to you, sir."

His eyes sparkled with delight. "Two days as my Servant."

"Okay, sir," I agreed shakily, realizing that this beautiful man was going to fuck me hard for all forty-eight hours that I was bound to him.

"You will tell me everything that I want to know once I have you impaled on the truth stick," he said grabbing his thick cock in his fist. It did not go unnoticed by me that his big hand could barely wrap around the thick shaft.

I swallowed hard and tried to sound just as confident as he did. "And you will sing like a lark when this tight ass is wrapped around your cock, milking you dry, sir."

"We shall see," he said with a grin. "And then?"

"And then, sir, I will see whether this might be something that could work for me . . . and for you."

"And if it doesn't work for you?"

I had to think about that for a couple of seconds. "I will leave, of course, and bother you no more, sir."

"And if you like being my Servant?" he smirked. There was no doubt in his mind at all that I would love being his sex slave.

"I will be yours to do with what you desire, sir," I said simply.

"And if I desire to bite you and make you one of us?"

I shrugged knowing that he could do this right now without my permission. "That will be your choice to make, sir."

He considered me for a full two minutes before saying anything. "When can we do this?"

"I just need to let people know where I will be and make some arrangements. How about in two days if it pleases you, sir?"

"Tomorrow," he said with finality.

"Okay, sir, tomorrow," I agreed like I had a choice.

"At sundown."

"Shall I report here, sir?"

The alpha leaned closer to me and said, "No." He lowered his head and took a huge intake of breath from my crotch to my face. He grinned broadly and said, "I will find you."

"And what do I call you?" I asked, feeling foolish.

He smiled a sly smile. "What every Servant calls his dominant."

"Master," I whispered as I bowed my head to him.

Chapter Nineteen

Part of a text string between Sutton Pike and his best friends held the next day:

I've never been drawn to a person like I was to him . . .
Just your type, Sutton?
It was more than just physical
I mean, yes, he was my type, but there was something else
What?
I'm not sure . . .
Was it his dominance over you?
Probably. I've never not been in control like that before . . .
Scary, huh?
Exhilarating!
He reminds me a little of Gray
That's good isn't it, because you really liked him?
And you are going to see him tonight?
Yes, can't wait!
What does Hawkes think about you being away for two days?
He doesn't like it!!

The day after my abduction, I slept until the late afternoon. Hawkes had to be dealt with when Ianu finally drove me home at five in the morning. I convinced my bodyguard to not cause trouble and then I had to tell him the whole story.

When I did wake up, I quickly showered and cleaned myself. I did not want to waste a second going with my new

Master when he finally showed up to get me. When my stomach started growling loud enough for others to hear, we decided to head to an outdoor café for dinner down the street in the old town square.

Hawkes and I ordered and were served pretty quickly. Starting to shovel the food into my mouth at first, I soon lost my appetite about half-way through the meal.

"You nervous?" my bodyguard asked me.

"Yes," I said simply.

"He means that much to you?" Hawkes was still trying to figure out what the hell had happened to me last night

"I'm not sure what he means to me, but I have to see if I can figure out what is wrong with me, and he seems to have some answers."

Hawkes smirked. "And it doesn't hurt that you want him to fuck you . . ."

"That never hurts," I said, laughing. "Although based on the size of his cock, it probably will hurt for a very long time afterwards."

"I'm going to the bathroom. You'll be okay for a minute?"

"I'll scream for help if anyone tries anything," I said with a smirk.

"Do that," Hawkes ordered, completely serious as he headed into the restaurant.

I sat on the heavy iron chair that was standard for this outside eating area and looked out into the gloaming light of twilight. There were quite a few people walking through the square and they suddenly seemed to move to the side. I watched in amazement as a car drove through the square right up to the fencing separating the restaurant's outdoor area from the rest of the walkway. The whole time that I had been in Romania, I had never seen a car on the square.

The car stopped near where I was sitting and I recognized it as a Bentley from the winged seal on the side panel. The car was silver and looked as if it had never been driven before.

I was shocked again when the alpha stepped out of the Bentley. His long strides had him at my table in a heartbeat. He was dressed in a very expensive silver suit coat over jeans and cowboy boots. His black dress shirt was adorned at the wrists with silver cufflinks but was wide open at the neck. Brown fur was visible between the starched linen panels. He was easily the hottest man in the city, but I could tell that he didn't care about that at all.

His smell arrived before he did—fresh pineapple and tennis balls. He was as disarming to me as I was to almost every NOMAR I had ever met in my life.

"How did you know I was here, Master?" I asked with incredulity as he approached my seat.

"Get in the car," he ordered.

"Hello to you also, Master."

The alpha wolf's icy blue eyes narrowed and his voice appeared inside my head. *"Don't make me punish you right here in front of all of these nice people. You know I will, little one. I don't give a fuck how special you are."*

I swallowed hard as I stood up. "I need to pay the check, sir."

"You are a Hound now. There is no need to pay," he informed me. My new Master reached in an inside pocket of his suit coat and produced the plain business card that I had seen before. He tossed it on the table and pointed at his car again. "What now?" he asked in frustration as he saw my inability to follow his directives.

"I have to tell my bodyguard, Master," I informed him.

"You may call him from the car and then I will take your phone and your clothes."

"Yes, sir." I felt the burn in my balls that signified that I was starting to get hard. I stood up and pushed my chair under the table. I wasn't immune to the distraction that we were causing, but I was delighted that the alpha was drawing just as much attention as I was. It was rare in my experience to have someone who drew more eyes to them than I did to myself.

Just as I was ducking to get into the car, I saw Hawkes at the table, looking in my direction. I waved to him and shook my cell phone at him. He nodded that he understood. I'm sure that he would be collecting as much information about the car and driver as he could before looking away.

"Are you even allowed to drive on the square, Master?" I asked once we were in the car. His smell had permeated the fine leather and fabric of the inside of the car.

"The first thing you are going to learn as my Servant is to not question me," he said gruffly. "Now, make your call to your bodyguard."

"Yes, Master."

"That did not require a response, Servant. You will be punished when I get you to my home."

Swallowing hard, I realized I was going to have to raise the level of my commitment to being subservient. I pushed Hawkes name on my smartphone and spoke to him. I assured him that I was okay and that I would see him late tomorrow night. I watched out the window as a policeman let us through a barricade guarding the square.

As soon as I disconnected the call, the alpha pulled the car over to the side of the road. He put his flashers on and said smoothly, "Give me your phone and take your clothes off."

"Right here, Master?" I asked in shock. I was grateful that in my surprise I had remembered to use his title.

"Are you questioning me again, special one?"

"Sorry, Master," I said quickly. Blushing, I handed this man my phone and then started to strip my clothes off. My new Master turned on the interior lights and watched every move I made as I removed all of my clothes and threw them into the back seat unceremoniously.

Master reached over and stopped my leg from nervously bouncing up and down by grabbing my thigh and squeezing. "Are you nervous, special one?"

"Yes, Master."

"You will relax when I have you where I want you," he said with a big grin as he put the car into gear and pulled back onto the road.

My cock was painfully hard and had been ever since I had seen my Master exit the car on the way towards me. His words now were not helping matters.

"I can see that you are happy to see me."

"Yes, Master, and I can see you are equally as happy to see me," I smirked as I nodded to the extremely big bulge in the front of his jeans.

"Surprisingly, I am," he admitted as he drove out of town and into the mountains.

We didn't speak again until we arrived at the Gothic mansion. I couldn't help but ask, "Is this your house, Master?"

"It is our house, special one."

"As in the pack, Master?"

"Exactly. Do not speak again until you are mounted on my cock," he commanded me.

I nodded to let him know that I understood and would try to be obedient.

"Try not to get pre-cum on my leather seat, special one."

I looked down and noticed that I was leaking golden man-goo all over myself. I made sure it wasn't on the seat as Master walked around the car and opened my door for me. I slid out of the car onto gravel and saw my cage waiting on me by the front door.

Master followed me over to the cage and picked up something off the top. It was a muzzle like you would use on a wild dog. A studded dog collar came next which Master promptly buckled around my neck.

"You have a question that you want to ask, special one?"

"Master wants to make sure that I do not escape?" I asked indicating my cage, muzzle, and collar with a hand.

"You are a Hound now and we follow the traditions very closely," he told me as he strapped the muzzle onto my face and buckled it into place. A piece of rubber pipe was held between my lips by the infernal contraption. "Now, shut up and get into the cage."

Master paraded me in my cage throughout the house again for everyone to see. I was the prize catch who had been captured and he was the victorious hunter. This time I saw Boris fucking some guy on all fours. Boris had been the man that started this whole thing for me. He was his hairy, muscled-self tonight just like the Boris that I had taken home and slept with that night a month ago before he changed physically in the morning.

As I finished being paraded through the ballroom, I wondered if these people had never left. Had they just fucked all night and all day? It made me feel badly for the men who were getting railed out until I remembered that they were probably deserving of punishment.

Master had me delivered to an enormous bedroom that contained the largest bed that I had ever seen. It must have been custom-made because it was bigger than any king-sized bed dreamed of being. The room was dark except for two small lamps on either side of the bed that barely illuminated it.

The man manipulating my cage stopped, lowered me to the floor, and left the room after bowing to the alpha. My Master slowly started to remove all of his clothes. I watched with unblinking wide eyes as his sexy body was revealed one piece of clothing at a time. He really was a remarkable man and everything about him let you know that.

I salivated as I watched him pull his cowboy boots off followed by his socks. I wanted nothing more than to be touching those masculine pads of his and to run my lips and tongue all over them. I could almost smell his muskiness from where I sat in my cage.

The alpha's pants and jock were the next to come off and his cock jumped out like a spear in a three-dimensional movie. The dark rings around his shaft made it look even more foreign than usual. He was so goddamn thick and long that even hard, his cock collapsed under its own weight and just arched slightly out of his crotch. It was the most intimidating and exciting prick that I had ever been in the same room with.

Master stood in front of me with his legs spread wide open. He was letting me drink in his body and I was binging myself on it like it was St. Patrick's Day and the green beer was free. Slowly, he opened the cage door.

"Come out, special one." His voice reverberated in every fiber of my being and pulsed in my hard cock like waves hitting the ocean.

I crawled out of my cage.

"Kneel to your Master," he commanded.

I followed his instructions immediately.

"I have waited longer for you than I've ever waited for any hole to fuck, little one. So, I'm going to let you suck me until I feed you my seed. And then I will start to train your ass. Nod if you understand, special one."

I nodded my muzzled head up and down. I was so excited that it felt like my heart was going to beat out of my chest.

"Good. Once I have you mounted on my cock, we can begin to get the answers to both of our questions."

Suddenly the questions he was speaking of were no longer in my head. The only thing I could think of was having him inside of me.

CHAPTER TWENTY

Partial list of infractions and punishments listed in the sacred texts of the Hounds:

Cheating at school: One night of submission
Fraud: Two nights of submission
Assault, resulting in non-injury: Three nights of submission
Assault, resulting in injury: Three nights of submission plus torture
Sex crimes: Three days and nights of torture
Identity theft: Three nights of submission
Theft: Two nights of submission
Arson: Three nights of submission plus torture
Drug charges: Two nights of submission and enrollment in treatment
Driving while impaired: Three nights of submission and torture
Murder: Three nights of submission and torture for twelve lunar cycles
Repeated offenses: Three nights of submission and authorities notified

Master moved the foam pad from the main floor up to the base of his chair. We had left the bedroom and returned to the throne room where he took a seat on his throne and snapped his fingers, pointing to the pad. I scrambled across the room, up the stairs, and knelt on the pad. Being this close to him was overwhelming my senses, making me feel dizzy and hot.

The alpha wolf reached down and unfastened the muzzle. He removed it and tossed it aside. "Let me see what I've got to work with, Servant," he gruffly commented.

In my experience, that usually meant that the NOMAR wanted to see my asshole, but my space was limited on this small top step, so I didn't know how to complete this task at first. He watched the look of confusion on my face with a smirk on his own until I figured it out.

I was going to have to do a handstand. Quickly getting into position before I had the chance to change my mind, I planted my hands on the pad and lifted my legs up into the air in front of the alpha wolf.

His rough hands spread my legs and thankfully also anchored me to him. The alpha wolf spread my ass cheeks with one big hand and massaged my puckered hole with the other. His body temperature heated my puckered hole just as effectively as if he had put a heating pad between my ass cheeks.

"It's pretty small, Servant. It will probably require more training than I first thought. So, are you ready for your punishment, little one?"

"Yes, Master," I answered, upside down.

The man who would be my new Master stood up, easily holding me by the ankles in front of him. I didn't feel insecure in his hands even for a second. I looked up at him and saw his erect cock blocking my sight.

"Tell me why I am forced to punish you, little one," he commanded me.

My head was swimming—between his overwhelming smell in my nose, his hot hands on my ankles, the looming view of his big cock in my eyes, and his complete and utter dominance over me, I was undone. "I was disrespectful, Master."

"How?" he asked as he reached down with one hand and retrieved a wooden paddle from beside his chair. I was amazed that he could so steadily hold me up with one arm like I weighed nothing.

"I didn't use your title of respect and questioned you in the car, Master," I gulped as I realized he was going to strike me with the paddle.

"Yes, you did," he agreed as his hand swung back.

Suddenly, his arm came forward and the paddle hit my ass cheeks with a crack and an explosion of pain. I had squeezed my eyes shut against the pain and now I felt the tears form in them. When another strike did not come immediately, I opened my eyes to see my Master looking down at me.

I blinked through my tears and noticed that a giant drop of golden man-goo was hanging off the end of his big Master cock. I badly wanted that drop of his essence inside my mouth. He held me suspended there until the drop of pre-cum became too heavy and landed squarely on my face.

"Do not let that pre-cum go in your mouth or on your lips, my Servant," he said firmly.

Fuck me! This Master was truly clever. The paddling was painful, but not something that I really cared about. It would not be a deterrent to my behavior, but not letting me taste him was absolute torture for me.

I was still in my head when the second strike of the paddle came. It was so hard that it pushed me forward and I had to fight to keep his pre-cum from moving onto my closed lips.

"I don't know what motivates you or what your limits are yet, Servant, but I will find out. I will punish you in the way that maximizes your change in behavior every single time that you disobey me. Do you understand?"

"Yes, Master," I said carefully, making sure to tilt my

head back so that his man honey did not run onto my lips.

"We shall see," he said as he threw the paddle to the floor. "You may taste me now, my Servant."

I quickly ran my tongue over my face to scoop the golden nectar into my mouth. He tasted like heaven!

Master held me steadily as he sat back down into his carved wooden chair. He lifted my legs and pulled my whole body back onto his. "Why don't you go ahead and get to know my cock a lot better while I do the same to your tiny hole?"

I didn't need to be asked twice to blow this man. Instead, I opened my mouth wide and swallowed the huge cockhead. It was coated with sticky pre-cum all the way down his wide shaft.

Master's skin tasted delicious and his man-honey was like the best dessert I had ever tasted. I couldn't get enough of it. I was disappointed that I could not get all of him inside my mouth, but I hadn't thought that there was really a chance of that anyway. Not only was Master one of the longest dicks I had ever sucked, but he was easily the widest, especially the closer to the base of his big monster you got. His skin was hot to the touch and we were both sweating like pigs as I lay on him.

The alpha wolf locked his massive arms around the small of my back and told me to keep my legs spread. My mouth was full of him when he lowered his bearded face into my crack and began to lick my rosebud. Good thing too, because I probably would have screamed if my mouth had been empty. My ass was so sensitive and Master's tongue and beard were relentless in their scratching and probing.

I had been rimmed while at the SA on multiple occasions, but not since because NOMARs were not normally into that kind of thing. I was not going to question it now, because it felt super-terrific especially when Master's tongue formed into a dart and entered me.

The alpha's tongue was probably much larger than most, so it genuinely felt like a small penis had entered me. Master worked his tongue back and forth like a Maestro working an orchestra. He was quite skilled at it, and the constant stretching of my anal ring had me on the edge of delirium.

I grabbed Master's cock by the base, trying to wrap both hands around it as I sucked. I began to take long drawing pulls off of him, my saliva running down the sides of his big shaft.

"It is more responsive to me than I first thought it would be, Servant," Master's deep voice rumbled throughout the room.

"I'm glad that you are pleased, Master," I said to him after pulling off of his juicy meat sword.

"I'm not even closed to pleased yet, Servant," he growled.

I watched in fascination as Master pulled a butt plug from beside him, wet it by sucking on it, and then pushed it against my puckered hole. It easily popped inside, splitting my anal ring and sending waves of pleasure coursing up my spinal cord.

I went back to sucking on his huge rod as he commented, "Wow, you have no problem with this size at all. Let's try something bigger."

Master continued to push bigger and bigger butt plugs into my ass as I sucked as much pre-cum out of his slobbering knob as I could. He seemed impressed with my asshole's ability to stretch and retract. He had switched from using his spit, to regular lube, and now had coated my ass in heavy petroleum jelly. Finally, he shoved a gigantic plug into me and marveled at how my anal ring wrapped around it.

"That's the biggest I have," he said deeply to me. He slowly rotated my body to the side until I was standing in front of him again. "Impressive, Servant, impressive."

When I opened my mouth to speak, I made a weird noise. The butt plug in my ass was considerably more present now that I was standing. I had to take a deep breath before trying to speak again. "Thank you, Master."

He looked at me with those icy blue eyes like he could see right through me. "It usually takes a month for me to train a new man to be able to take me, but you might just be ready now. What do you say?"

"I am ready now, Master," I told him as I knelt back down on the pad and resumed sucking his pole.

"We shall see about that, Servant."

I pulled off of him again and sat back on my heels painfully.

"You want to ask your Master something, little one?

I nodded and he indicated for me to speak. I asked, "You said that you were going to answer my questions once I was mounted on your cock, Master."

"Yes. What's your point, Servant?"

"So, you were going to wait a month or more to answer me?"

"Yes." His beautiful lips smirked and his eyes danced with delight at his deception. "You have a problem with that?"

"Yes, Master," I repeated his plain answer.

He chuckled. "Maybe you will surprise me tonight."

"Hopefully," I admitted. "I want to be riding your pole as soon as possible, sir."

"I like your ambition, Servant. Shall we begin?"

"Yes, Master."

"Put my cock back into your mouth," he commanded.

Dropping to my knees, I could feel every inch of that butt plug stretching me almost to my limits. I shifted uncomfortably trying to find some relief before unhinging my jaw and trying to consume my new Master's fuck stick.

"Is that the furthest you can go, Servant?"

I nodded as I gagged myself on his massive pole.

Master used his pointer finger to mark on his cock where my lips were. "Remove your mouth," he ordered.

I pulled off of him and watched as he held his finger in place. It was just slightly past the first tattooed dark ring around his shaft.

"Tell me the letters on the bottom of my cock that correspond to this ring, Servant," his deep voice boomed at me.

I was confused at first but slowly lifted his big meat to see that the rings on the bottom side of his shaft had small neatly printed letters on them.

I read them aloud to him as I read them myself. "N . . . S . . . S, Master."

"Hmmm," he said to himself, obviously enjoying knowing something that I did not.

I sat back on my heels and waited. I was being far more patient with this man than I was used to being—maybe it was the huge butt plug stretching my anal ring out or maybe it was the fact that I was desperate to please him.

"NSS, not so special, Servant," he told me, his lips turning up into a smirk. "What have you to say for yourself?"

"I'm sorry, Master," I said quickly, feeling bad that I had disappointed him already. I did find it amazing that someone had reached the second ring on his shaft and unbelievable that anyone had impaled themselves all the way down to the third ring.

"I don't care about your sorrow, Servant. I want the best from you, so you will get better and show me. Tell me."

"Yes, Master."

"Show me," he commanded. Master's voice was so deep and gravelly that I knew he was in full lust mode right now. I took advantage of that and gave him my very best blowjob.

As I relaxed and got into the rhythm of sucking my new

Master off, I was able to take more of him down my throat. He seemed pleased with me as he grabbed my head and groaned his approval. I pulled on his large ball sack that was swinging between his legs as I pumped my mouth back and forth over his hard shaft.

"Fuck, I'm gonna cum," he growled down at me.

I made a humming noise of approval as I continued to work him over. Most guys would have stopped and prepared, but I wanted this man to be pleased with me more than anything, so I kept going.

I was rewarded with a bear-like growl from Master as the cum vent on the top of his cock opened and released a torrent of scalding hot cum into my mouth and throat. I swallowed as fast and as often as I could, but there was no way I could keep up with the flow as strand after strand of sticky man-goo hit me in the back of the throat.

"Fuuuccccckkkkkk!" Master growled.

White frothy man juice poured out of both sides of my mouth as I continued to work my mouth up and down my Master's shaft. I had swallowed enough of his seed to know that it was definitely something that I wanted to keep eating.

It felt like Master's nut juice would never stop flowing, but I soon had swallowed a belly full and cleaned up his rod for him. I sat back on my heels and looked up into his handsome face, waiting for his next command.

He reached down with an over-sized paw and stroked the side of my face. "That was pretty good, Servant. Not the best I've ever had, but not bad."

"Thank you, Master," I said with more than a little sarcasm dripping from my lips.

"Careful, little one, I will go to the ballroom and bring one of those criminals in here and fuck him until dawn while you watch if you are not careful," he growled.

Fuck! I don't want that. "Sorry, Master," I said quickly.

"I knew that I should have just bitten you and got it over with," Master smirked as I stared at him, dry mouthed.

Chapter Twenty-One

Part of a letter from the alpha of Romania to one of the alphas in the United States written on the morning of the eighth of June and overnight-delivered later that day:

Hello Father,

I know that I have not been in contact recently or often, but something has come to my attention that I need your help with in order to proceed. Your years of experience will be valuable in this case and if you don't mind sharing your thoughts with me, I would appreciate it greatly.

Several weeks ago, some of my pack was playing in a football game in the National Stadium. We were using pack talk to communicate with each other during the game . . . yes, father, I know we should not cheat, but it requires too much concentration to not use it when exerting athletically.

Towards the end of the game, we became aware that someone else in the stadium was communicating with us. I knew immediately that it was not one of my boys, but I was not at an angle to see who it was. My Hounds on the field said that it was a marked man in one of the skyboxes, but he shrunk from view as soon as he realized that we had heard him.

Have you ever heard of a wolf from another pack who could communicate with an opposing pack? How about a marked man being a wolf? I remember you telling me that marked men have been bitten by our kind in the past, but they have not turned.

I directed the Hounds to conduct a search of Bucharest and we were finally able to find and apprehend him. He claims to be special, and I have to admit that I've never seen anyone like him. He

144

has agreed to be my Servant for the weekend.

"Let me see that asshole again, Servant," my new Master ordered.

I did another handstand and dropped my legs onto his shoulders as the alpha wolf sat in his chair. He pulled the butt plug out of my ass, giving me an immediate sensation of relief followed by a feeling of emptiness.

"You might be the rare man that I don't have to train very much in order to ride my cock, Servant." Master had inserted both thumbs into my asshole and was now stretching it out to get a good look at it. "What do you think about that?"

"I hope so, Master," I said from upside-down.

"You want to give it a shot?"

"Yes, Master."

"Very well," he said, like it was a chore he was committing to. The big man helped me rotate back to my feet.

I stood in front of him as I watched the alpha press a button on his chair and the arms descended into the floor. His icy blue eyes dared me to comment, but I was too enamored with him to say a word. He reached beside him and produced a tub of petroleum jelly which he rubbed generously over the top of his knob.

Master arched an eyebrow at me and pointed to the second tattooed line on his big shaft.

I nodded my head up and down with confidence.

He made a face of disbelief but began to rub the jelly between the first and second lines. I reached forward and moved his hand even lower, drawing a stern look of disbelief from him.

"Don't waste my time, little one," he warned me. "You truly think that you are special, don't you?"

"I guarantee you that being in my ass will not be a waste of your time, Master."

"It is time to see if your ass can deliver what your mouth has promised, Servant."

I nodded instead of speaking.

"Climb up here, Servant."

I awkwardly climbed up onto the throne chair with Master's help. He held his massive cock up by wrapping his hand around the base while I pointed the lubed cock head at my asshole. Some days I had complete confidence in my ability to take a large cock and some days I didn't. I was extremely fortunate that today I felt like I could slide down a flagpole and not get hurt. I've never been sure why some days were different than others, but facing Master's giant babymaker made me happy that today was the day that I was confident.

Closing my eyes, I held my breath as the velvety soft head of his cock touched my puckered hole. Willing myself to lower down onto him, I felt his cock head push through my skin and then the tremendous joy of my anal ring being stretched wide to accommodate first the head and then the shaft. My ass continued to stretch further and further as I slid down his big monster.

It felt like I couldn't stretch any wider as I reached the halfway point to being on Master's lap. He had a look like he was impressed on his face as he said, "You easily hit that first mark, Servant."

"I aim to please, Master."

"Humph. I will be the judge of my pleasure once I see whether you are as special as you claim to be, little one. And I will have to punish you again for speaking out of turn. You know that, right?"

"Yes, Master." I blew a deep breath out and bore down on him again. Willing myself to relax, I moved further down that meat flag pole. I had never felt so full of man meat before and the sensation was incredible. The pain was like having a hot knife shoved inside you, but the pleasure offset some of the discomfort. In one brief moment of panic, I wondered if I might have torn something inside me or whether I would tear something, but I quickly dismissed it as wave after wave of pleasure overflowed my brain stem.

Master took a small sharp intake of breath as I passed the second tattooed line on his cock. "That one is marked SS for somewhat special, Servant. You think you have done something?"

I smiled, knowing that I was winning him over. "I call it two-thirds of the way there, Master."

"You're not . . ." he started.

"I am," I said confidently, even though I wasn't at all. My ass already felt like it was at max capacity and there was more to go, but now I was determined. Determined to see if I could do it and determined to prove to this man that I was special.

"Not only speaking out of turn but now interrupting your Master. Is this how you want to test me, boy?"

"No, sir." Blowing out several big breaths, I went to my happy place in my mind and continued to lower myself onto the fat appendage that seemed to have been made to fuck one hole. I was going to prove that hole belonged to me. Before I even realized what was happening, I slid the rest of the way down and was sitting in the Master's lap. His big bush of brown pubic hair made a soft nest for me to come to rest upon. This man who considered himself a werewolf was now touching places inside me that no man had ever reached before.

"Well, god damn!" he said in awe. "There is something special about you, after all, my Servant."

It did not go unnoticed by me that for the first time he had addressed me as *my Servant*. I took a deep breath and smiled up into his handsome face.

"You are the first person to ever do that without several months of training," he said quietly. "Speak to me."

"I've been training for this my whole life, Master," I told him as I reveled in the incredible feeling of fullness that I was getting from him. I had thought that I had felt this feeling before, but it was nothing compared to what was happening right now.

Absentmindedly, I reached up to his face and ran my hand over his long brown beard. His icy blue eyes watched me with curiosity as I studied his face. He had a scar across the bridge of his nose that my fingertips found and the cutest little ears that were attached close to his head. I ran my fingers through his hair pushing it away from his part.

"You approve, little one?" he asked softly.

I nodded up and down while looking deep into his eyes. *Is this the man for me? Is he the Master I've always dreamed of?* I had never experienced this combination of sheer pleasure and abject pain before and I was enthralled by it.

When my Master spoke next, his voice was huskier than I had ever heard it. "I'm going to fuck you hard now and then we will talk."

I swallowed hard. *"Yes, Master."*

His icy blue eyes never left my green ones as he reached under each of my thighs and held my ass right in place. Master undulated his crotch, slowly pulling that big blue-veiner out of me and then equally as slowly, he pushed it back in up to the hilt.

"Amazing,"

I wrapped my arms around his thick biceps and hung onto him. His breathing and his heartbeat were just as steady as when I had been talking to him, seemingly unresponsive to my talents. His smell was so strong this close to him and I breathed in deeply to fill my sinus cavity with it. Heat poured off both of our bodies like we were in the middle of the Sahara.

Master's slow start had me panting and sweating in no time at all. Almost as if he could read my thoughts, he increased his speed and his depth. Beginning to move me up and down along with his crotch doing the same thing, I was soon slamming into him over and over as he gave me one of the most complete fucks that I had ever experienced.

"Master," I thought to him.

"Servant," he thought back.

"Your cock is amazing, my Master."

"Your sweet hole is tight as fuck, my Servant."

"You will ruin me for everyone else, Master."

"I hope so, little one."

I knew it was true. Once I felt Master's dick inside me and the way that it so completely filled me and fit inside me like it was made to go there, I knew that I would never be satisfied with another. I wanted to close my eyes, throw my head back, and writhe in unabashed hedonistic pleasure on top of his over-sized fun organ, but I couldn't look away from his eyes.

They were so compelling to me and the faster he fucked into me the deeper I fell into his eyes. The sides of his cute little lips started to turn upwards in a smirk as he reached jackhammer speed. He was fucking destroying my ass.

I squeezed his tatted biceps and felt the power inside them. Using one hand, I released his arm and ran it over his ripped chest. I stopped to pinch each of his rock-hard nipples, enjoying the sharp intakes of breath that it caused my new Master. My own cock was now hard as shit and was being whipped between hitting my stomach and smashing down on Master's washboard abs with each down-thrust. I could feel my climax building and knew that it was only a matter of moments before I would explode.

"Fucking me hard, Master."

"Fucking you the way you need fucked, Servant."

"I need it."

"You need me."

"I need you, Master."

"Show me how much, little one."

"I'm going to cum, Master."

My eyelids fluttered shut as I reached the edge of my orgasm and then fell over the cliff. Master held me still with his big cock firmly planted inside me—every single inch of his manhood wrapped by my hot flesh. His big cock had destroyed my prostate by pounding it into submission over and over and now throbbed inside me like a ticking time bomb.

The alpha wolf reached down and pointed the head of my cock at his washboard stomach. His touch was the last thing that I needed to send me into the stratosphere, so my cum vent opened and I shot strand after strand of hot sticky spunk onto his beautifully chiseled chest and stomach. Wrapping his hand around my hard shaft, he milked more of my sweet cream out of my dick.

I moaned shamelessly as my asshole tightened around his thick shaft, threatening to strangle him. I had never felt such pleasure before and I was overloaded with it. When I opened my eyes, Master was smirking at me.

"Now the real fuck can begin, my Servant."

"Master."

"I will replace your cum with my own and then you will belong to us."

"I already belong to you, Master."

"I'm not sure what you are, my Servant, but your ass is unlike any that I have ever fucked before."

"Same for your cock, Master."

"We shall have to test your limits."

"Do with me what you wish, Master."

"I wish to tear you asunder."

I felt like he already had. Focusing on his eyes again, I

pumped my legs up and down causing my ass to speedily fly up and down his thick shaft. He smiled, let go of my ass cheeks, folded his arms behind his head, and interlocked his fingers while I took over. This gave me a great view of his flexed biceps and hairy armpits, and I could feel the blood rushing back to the spongy areas of my limp cock.

My thighs were beginning to burn, and my asshole felt like it was on fire. Finally collapsing onto his lap, I leaned forward and buried my mouth into his left armpit. I licked, bit, and chewed his sweaty hairy fold of skin, savoring his salty perspiration.

Master used his free arm to wrap around my waist and hold me in the small of my back. He held me stationary as he fucking drilled me from below. He pushed my head back from his armpit as he reached his climax. My new Master continued to thrust even as he began to fill my ass with his hot seed. I didn't know where his cum was going to go, because I couldn't possibly have any more room inside me.

"Fuuuucccccckkkkkk!" Master growled through clenched teeth, sending a coating of hot saliva onto my face.

His forceful thrusts produced a series of grunts and groans from him. His technique soon started to falter until he completely disassembled and lost himself in his release.

The man who had been a stranger to me yesterday, but now I recognized as my true Master, opened his eyes and stared at me with his head slightly tilted down. He tilted his head back and instinctively I did the same thing. Without even a thought transferring between us, we both put our heads all the way back, opened our mouths, and howled loudly.

The reception hall was still echoing with our howls when the flood of thoughts from the other wolves flooded my brain.

"What the fuck is going on in there?"

"The alpha has conquered the marked wolf."

"I've never heard a sound like that."

"It is the sound of the alpha meeting his match."

"The alpha will figure the marked one out and will tell us."

"Sounds like he is busy figuring him out now!"

"I was wrong, little one," Master whispered to me once the other's thoughts had settled.

I looked at him with a questioning visage.

"I'm going to need to do that one more time before we talk," he said with a smile that revealed a beautiful set of white teeth.

I returned his smile. "I am yours, Master. Do with me what you desire."

"You no longer want answers to your questions?" He pushed a button and the arms on his chair rose back into place.

"I do, but I am willing to let you give them to me on your time now."

"And why is that, my Servant?"

"Because I belong to you now, Master. I trust that you will tell me what I need to know."

Master picked me up and stood with me easily. He walked down the stairs and said, "Grab the piece of foam, Servant." He lowered me down so that I could reach it before he climbed the stairs again. "Put it in the chair."

I placed the foam onto the chair and the alpha wolf lowered my back on top of it. He lifted my legs up onto the arms of the big throne chair and pulled my ass to the front edge of the seat. His cock had never come out of me or diminished in size the whole time, so when he began to try to saw me in half with it again, I was thrilled out of my mind.

"You are mine."

"I am yours, Master."

CHAPTER TWENTY-TWO

A partial list of the districts covered by various packs, as listed in the sacred documents of the Hounds library:

Hounds of Budapest- Romania, Hungary, Moldova, Ukraine, Belarus

The Punishers- Alaska, Canada, Greenland, Iceland

The Plague- Russia

Dogs of Death- Mexico & Central America

Pride Pack- Brazil & Southern South America

Cheyenne Coyotes- Midwest USA

Wild Dogs of Borneo- India, Pakistan, Afganistan, Iran, Iraq

Werewolves of London- United Kingdom, Scandinavia

Lycan It, Loving It- Western USA

Hell's Bitches- Caribbean Islands

The Lupine- Japan, Korea, China, Hong Kong, Thailand, Indonesia, Vietnam

Canine Criminals- Australia, New Zealand, Pacific Islands

Jackals- Egypt, Libya, Algeria, Sudan, Chad, Niger, Mali, Yemen, Ethiopia

Carnivores of Cannes- France, Spain, Portugal

The Sight- Germany, Austria, Switzerland, Liechtenstein, Belgium

The Carnage- Italy, Greece, Turkey, Slovenia, Slovakia, Czech Republic

The alpha wolf had just given me the two best fucks of my life. I had never met a man that I had such an immediate connection to before. He reminded me of Gray in the fact that I had an instant physical connection to him and the way he domineered me. I had been really lucky to have had these last two experiences with them.

"God damn!" the man who was my new Master finally exclaimed once he had regained the ability to talk. I was still stretched out on his throne chair and his fat cock was still firmly planted inside me. He had dumped a tremendous amount of hot man-cream into my ass and now it was starting to sluice out of me with each one of his movements.

His icy blue eyes sparkled at me as he said, "I was wrong to mock you, Servant. There is something very special about you."

"And what is that, Master?" I asked, knowing the answer already.

He smirked and said, "Well, first of all, I have never seen anyone take my cock like that on the first try. And secondly, your sweet hole was just as tight for me the second fuck as the first. How did you do that?"

"It is a special gift of mine, sir," I admitted.

"We need to talk. Mind if we go somewhere more comfortable?"

"I am yours to command, Master."

Master growled instead of answering. Reaching under my back, he lifted me up into the air on powerful legs and easily descended the steps. I wrapped my arms around his thick neck and enjoyed being so close to him.

The alpha wolf stepped up to a carved wooden panel and opened his mouth against a panel on the wall. A hidden door smoothly slid open and my Master carried us inside. This room was the circular bedroom dominated by the giant bed I had seen when I first arrived here. The smell of fresh pineapple and new tennis balls was overwhelming in this room and I breathed in deeply trying to fill myself with it.

Master easily stepped onto the bed and sat down with his back against the heavy wooden headboard. I settled down onto his lap, making sure that his big cock was firmly planted inside my sore ass. His hypnotic eyes never left mine as I ground my ass onto his crotch, feeling fuller than ever before.

"I'm going to keep you filled with my big dick while we talk, Servant. You will be able to talk freely with me during this time."

"I would like that, Master. Both the talking and your cock inside me." I marveled at his stamina. Not only had he just cum three times, but he had not even needed any recovery time in between. This might just be the man for me after all. "How will this work, Master?"

"I will ask you a question and you will answer honestly. If I feel like you have, I will allow you to ask me a question."

"And you will answer honestly, Master?"

"Yes, little one."

"Okay, Master." I was thrilled that the time had come when I was hopefully going to get some answers.

"I have your permission now, my Servant?"

I kept quiet, knowing there was no way to answer this without more punishment.

"I thought so," he said with confidence. "When did the voices begin, Servant?" The penetration of his eyes into my soul let me know that there was no way that I could lie to this man in my current position.

"They began right after I got fucked by a guy I had picked up one night, Master." I was careful not to use Boris' name because I didn't want to get him into trouble.

"Yes. It was Boris, was it not?"

"Yes, Master," I admitted.

"And you had not heard the voices before that?"

"It was a buzzing in my head before that, Master. Almost

like I had a radio on, but it had not been tuned into a station yet."

"Okay. You may ask me a question now, Servant."

"What are the Hounds?" In my haste for answers, I had forgotten to use his title. He growled to let me know and his cock throbbed inside of me.

"It is the name of our pack."

"Pack of werewolves, Master?" I ventured.

"Yes, little one," he said, matter-of-factly.

"And you have never been bitten by one of us before, Servant?" he asked in all seriousness.

"Not that I'm aware of, Master."

"You would know, little one. You may ask me another question."

"You actually turn into wolves, Master?" I asked, feeling my eyes widening even though I tried not to let them.

Master took such a deep breath that I instinctively reached down and placed the palm of one of my hands on his chest. His eyes burned for me and my ass returned the burn back to him. "We have lost the ability to actually change all the way," he finally admitted as he broke our gaze. I could see that this pained him to admit to me.

I wasn't sure what to say to that. *Are these just guys who pretend to be werewolves but are unable ever to prove it? If so, it's really convenient.* I finally asked, "But you change some of the way, Master?"

"As you know when you saw Boris change in the morning, Servant. Now, it's my turn. Besides smelling somewhat like a wolf, running hot, and hearing our pack talk, what other special skills do you have, little one?"

I had to think about that for a couple of seconds because I had never even considered the things I could do as having a supernatural reason. "I do have a very strong sense of smell, Master."

He immediately perked up and his big cock throbbed

away inside me. "How strong?"

"I can identify people by their smell, Master."

"If you walk into a room, could you tell how many people are there by smell?" he carefully asked.

"Yes, sir."

My new Master raised his eyebrows in surprise. "What do I smell like to you, little one?"

I blushed furiously.

"Tell me," he commanded. His cock became even more insistent inside me.

"You smell like my two favorite smells, Master." He didn't say anything, but the ends of his lips twitched and his eyes commanded me to speak again. "Fresh pineapple and new tennis balls, Master."

Master lifted my arm to his nose and inhaled. Lowering my arm, he said, "You smell like sex to me, Servant."

I blushed even more furiously, feeling it on my neck and ears.

"Which is my favorite smell," he admitted with smiling lips behind his heavy beard. "Any other special talents?"

"I can speak and read languages that I have never studied before."

Master nodded. "Anything else?"

"Just the one that you are currently enjoying, Master."

"And enjoying it, I am," he said as he thrust into me several more times with emphasis. "I believe it is your turn, little one."

I thought for a second. "What does your pack do then if you can't change into wolves, Master?"

"We are very affluent people in our regular lives, Servant. We specialize in careers that involve communication and power — lawyers, professional athletes, politicians, police, government agencies, television news anchors, and personal trainers."

I was impressed. "What do you do, Master?"

"I fuck sweet little asses like yours, Servant."

The flush of my skin continued to any area not already covered. I tried to cover by asking another question. "Can you turn anytime you like, Master?"

"Only on the full moon—which is about three days every month. Now, it's my turn."

"Yes, sir," I said as my next question annoyingly popped into my head once it was not my turn.

"What are you doing here in Romania, little one?"

Just the fact that he called me by this nickname made my balls tingle and the blood rush to my dick. I had been bigger than most people my whole life and had never had anyone call me little before. But sitting on this big man's lap with the largest cock inside me that I had ever ridden, I knew he could call me whatever he wanted to call me.

"I followed someone, Master."

"A NOMAR?"

"Yes, sir."

"And where is he now, Servant?"

I easily admitted, "It didn't work out, Master."

"Shame. What kind of fool would let you go?"

I smiled at his compliment but did not answer him.

"Your turn, little one," he told me with a husky tone.

"What happened to Boris, Master?"

The alpha wolf's eyes sparkled with delight. "He was punished for not telling us that he had fucked you, little one."

"Oh."

"Boris did not want to admit that he had broken the rules by letting you see him the morning after a full moon. He knew where you were the whole time we were searching for you, Servant, and he kept your secret."

"You didn't kill him, did you, Master?" I asked before

holding my breath.

Master chuckled. "No, Sutton, I did not kill him. We are in the punishment business. Every full moon, we punish men who have done evil, including Boris."

"By fucking them, Master?"

"Among other things," he said secretively. "You would be amazed at what a deterrent it is, little one."

I leaned into his broad chest and put my hand up onto his bearded jaw. "You won't look like this in two days, Master?" I rocked my ass back and forth, making his big cock move inside me impressively.

He smiled broadly and answered, "No, but I'm sure that I will still be able to satisfy you, little one."

"I'm sure of that, as well, Master," I said, feeling the heat blossom on my skin again. *How can he stay hard for so long?*

"One last question, my Servant, can we just go ahead and say that you will be mine from now on?"

I had only agreed to give this a trial for two days, and we were barely two hours into it, but I knew the answer already, so there was no need to be coy about it. "Yes, Master."

CHAPTER TWENTY-THREE

A partial list of the members of the Hounds as of the summer of 2015:

Hound, Age, Occupation
Alpha, 35, Pack Master
Beta, 34, Military
Gamma, 47, Chief of Police
Delta, 52, Judge
Epsilon, 45, Lawyer
Zeta, 41, Representative
Eta, 41, Mayor
Theta, 36, Lawyer
Iota, 29, Detective
Kappa, 25, Ceo-Telecom
Lambda, 24, News Anchor
Mu, 22, Policeman
Nu, 21, Football Player
Xi, 21, Night Club Owner
Omicron, 20, Football Player
Pi, 20, Military
Rho, 19, Football Player

Master took a small break by fucking my brains out twice more while I lay under him, holding onto his big biceps. He was able to produce wave after wave of pleasure that coursed throughout my body. His giant cock was destroying my prostate both on the thrusts inside me and then by smashing it when he had my ass fully impaled.

I came just by the friction of Master's hairy abs against my hard prick on each thrust. He growled his satisfaction at the tighter hole that I presented to him afterwards. My asshole was burning so much that I wondered if I was doing major damage to myself, but I didn't want him to stop. I did wonder how long he was going to be able to keep this up.

The alpha wolf pulled his big phallus out of me and turned me onto my side facing away from him. The man that had dominated me this night like no other man ever had in my life lay down behind me. He lifted my leg onto his hip and fed his big dick back inside me. Unbelievably, he was still hard and not sated.

I closed my eyes and rode the rhythmic thrusts of my new Master. I enjoyed having his big body spooned up against my back and his muscled arm clamped onto my chest, holding me in place.

I wasn't sure when I fell asleep, but I woke sometime later hearing Master softly snore behind me. We were in the same position that I last remembered — his cock in my ass, his arm around my chest, our bodies spooned together. I fell right to sleep again warmed by his big body next to mine.

Sunlight was streaming through the high windows of the alpha's bedchamber when I woke next. His cock was still firmly planted in my ass, and we had not moved a single inch since falling asleep. It felt like I had a telephone pole rammed inside of me and my ass hurt like hell.

"I'm going to rail you out one more time, my Servant, and then I will clean us up," Master's deep voice boomed right behind my ear. "I know you are probably sore and need to rest."

"Yes, Master," I said with a cracking morning voice. I wanted to brush my teeth badly.

"On all fours, little one, and don't you dare let my cock come out of you," he commanded.

It was a difficult assignment that was made easier by the fact that he was so long. It was really hard for him to come all the way out of me and I was soon on my hands and knees in front of the big man. And even though my ass was on fire and I felt like I would die if he fucked me again, I pushed my ass back towards him so that I would be full of him again.

Master fucked me long and slow. He kept his hands on my hips and used them to drive me back and forth on his enormous cock. That giant laphog felt twice as big as it had last night and I moaned shamelessly as he fucking drilled me with it.

"Fuuuuccccckkkkkk," the big werewolf groaned behind me. "How the shit is your fucking hole so damn tight around my cock?"

I was wondering the same exact thing. He had kept my hole stretched out around his thick girth for the entire night and part of the morning.

"I've fucking filled you up for hours now. No one I've ever fucked has been able to return from that," he said in disbelief. "How are you doing that?"

"I could ask the same thing about your hard cock, Master," I moaned in front of him as he repeatedly mangled my prostate.

"I'm going to fucking tear you up," he growled as he redoubled his efforts and gave me a fucking for the record books. We both came within seconds of each other and collapsed in exhaustion onto the bed.

"Little one," Master said lazily after he regained his breath. "I see now that you are very special and you are mine."

"I am yours, Master," I said into the mattress.

The alpha wolf blew out a deep breath and pulled his thick cock out of my sore ass for the first time in a very long time. The feeling of emptiness flooded my brain shortly after the feeling of relief did. My ass felt weird, like it was waiting for his cock to go back to its' now-normal resting space.

I felt Master's hands under my neck and knees. He was picking me up and seemed to be doing it effortlessly. Master carried me to an open door and into a huge bathroom. It was completely made out of dark slate and soapstone. He carried me down into one of two big pools cut into the floor.

The water was warm and it felt like heaven on my sore ass and muscles. Surprising me with his gentleness, the alpha werewolf sat down on a submerged seat and sat me on his lap. There was a wicker basket near us on the slate and my new Master reached inside it and produced a sponge and a bottle of soap.

Master slowly poured the liquid soap on the sponge and then gently started to scrub my skin. I couldn't look away from his face as he concentrated on cleaning me. When he lifted his eyes, I saw that he considered me as his possession already. It made my breath catch in my throat and my face flush immediately

"I will always take care of you, little one," he said in explanation.

"Thank you, Master."

The alpha wolf slowly turned me over and meticulously cleaned my ass and back. He didn't have a shower wand to clean out my insides, but he did the best he could with his long fingers. He also cleaned his own crotch. Once he considered me clean, my new Master flipped me back over before picking me back up into his arms. He steadily lifted us out of the pool and walked over to the other, much larger, pool.

This one was a hot tub. The largest most elegant hot tub I

had ever seen. The water burned my skin at first and then felt amazing. There were two strange holes on opposite sides of the pool.

Master submerged both of us in the giant hot tub to wash the soap off of us before holding me back out of the water. "You will soak here until I return, Servant."

"You have to leave, Master?"

"Yes. I have some pack business to take care of and you will wait here for me," he said firmly. "Do you understand?"

"Yes, Master."

"You can put your head into those holes and float without worrying about anything," he informed me as he stood up, water running off of his amazing body.

I stared in obvious lust for him.

He smirked at my glazed over look. "I will give you a hard fuck when I finish and then we will go to bed, little one," he stated matter-of-factly.

I swallowed hard and nodded my head as I watched him dry his body with a giant fluffy towel and then he was gone. I examined the holes for floating in the side of the pool. They were raised higher than the water line so they were mostly dry and lined with a heavy black rubber.

Lowering my head down, my neck fit into the opening against the side and I saw the logic in that my head would not be able to slip through. I lifted my feet and began to float. It was heavenly and the hot water and bubbles made my sore ass feel almost normal again.

I must have fallen asleep, because I woke with a start. Master was beside me in the hot tub. His strong arms and hands reached under me and lifted me out. He had a towel draped over his shoulder as he carried me out to his bed. Master gently laid me on the bed and began to dry me before he dried himself.

The alpha wolf crawled up onto the bed with me and

grabbed the tube of lube from our earlier fucks.

"How would Master like me this time?"

"Master would like you silent. I will move you wherever you need to be for my pleasure, Servant."

Shit! He isn't happy. Has something gone wrong with the pack while I was soaking in the tub? He wanted me to be quiet, so I wasn't even able to ask him.

True to his word, my Master flipped me over onto my stomach and pulled me to the corner of the bed. He had me lay over the corner and he easily mounted me in this position. I tried to stay silent, but I couldn't stop a huge moan from escaping my lips when he plowed completely into me.

Master was so big and so thick that each time he entered me I got the feeling it was never going to happen. He stretched my anal ring out so far that I thought for sure he was doing major damage to me. But he didn't, instead choosing to pry me open like a clam shell and depositing his pearl deep into my guts.

"Fuuuuccccckkkkkk!" the big guy groaned as he hit his release. "Your fucking hole is so tight." He had one hand on the small of my back pressing me down into the mattress which lifted my ass into the air. The other hand was pressing down on my face as I lay with my cheek against the bed. It was a position of dominance and I was thrilled that he was sharing it with me.

The alpha wolf continued to thrust his giant rod into me over and over, even after cumming. I loved how this man fucked, and I already knew that I would be very happy lying under him for as long as he would have me. My mind raced about how I could make that happen.

I was still lost in my head scheming when Master returned to himself and lifted off me. Pulling his still mostly erect dick out of me, he said, "I don't think I can let you go after this full moon, little one."

Keenly aware that he wanted me not to speak, I did not

tell him that I felt the same way towards him. I surprised myself even admitting that to myself. I had never felt so strongly about a man with whom I had slept with already, not even Gray. It was scary and emotional.

Master bent down, flipped me over, and easily lifted me into his arms. He laid me down like a baby on the side of the bed with my head on the pillows. He lay down beside me and pulled the sheet over us. We wouldn't need anything more since we were both throwing off a tremendous amount of body heat.

"We will sleep for most of the day, little one. When you wake, you will give me a blowjob before I give you another hard fucking. Do you understand?"

"Yes, Master."

He smiled. "And then I will be very pleased with you, my Servant."

Unbelievably, I wanted nothing more than to please this man who I had just met but had already committed myself to.

CHAPTER TWENTY-FOUR

Excerpt from an official police report filed by a Bulgarian national in the summer of two thousand and fifteen in Sophia, Bulgaria:

Victim reports that he was abducted from his home on July twentieth. He was home alone around ten o'clock at night when his doorbell rang. He says three men immediately accosted him. They put a black hood over his head and restrained his arms and legs.

Curiously, the suspects stopped and secured the victim's house before leaving. When a friend went to check on him, he found the front door closed and locked. All signs of struggle had been cleaned up.

Victim reports that he was carried across the border into Romania with others in the back of a tanker truck. Once in Romania, he was caged along with at least twenty others, each in their individual cages in a mansion. He assumes that it was Romania based on the language of the captors. He was fed and given water regularly.

For three nights, the victim says he was brutally assaulted, both sexually and emotionally. He was raped by multiple men and forced to give them oral sex. During the day, they kept him caged.

The victim's captors said that this was his punishment for crimes that he had committed, which he denies. They informed him that if he told anyone, they would be back and he believed them. No medical evidence was found in the Emergency Room report that would corroborate his testimony. Victim claims this is due to a very intensive cleaning process that his captors used.

Victim is currently being charged with grand theft auto. He claims that he had to steal the car in order to flee the country and get away from the men who did this to him. At this point he is not credible, due to the overwhelming evidence against him. Case closed.

True to his word, my new Master had blown a load down my throat and then fucked me hard and fast after we woke from our rest. I was in awe of his fucking skills, his stamina, and his command over me. I had never met anyone like him before and my mind was racing a million miles an hour, trying to figure out how I was going to make him mine.

Master once again washed and dried us both in the cleaning pool of his bathroom. He let me brush my teeth and use the restroom before he called for me from the bedroom.

"Yes, Master?" I hurried to him.

He was sitting on the bed surrounded by gadgets. "Turn around, my Servant."

I did and he began to strap a chain onto my dog collar. It went to a large metal ring that sat flat on the middle of my chest and then continued down. I could feel another heavy chain running down my spine. Separate chains connected the back one to the ring on my chest.

"Turn," he ordered again.

I spun back to him and watched in amazement as he put a black leather cuff on the shaft of my hard cock and secured it with a Velcro strap. He attached the chain to the cuff and used a dangling piece of leather to wrap my balls up towards the cuff.

"Hands above your head and spread your legs, little one."

I lifted my arms and spread my legs. He connected the back chain under my grundle to the cuff on my penis. I felt totally strapped down, even though the chains barely covered any part of me. Everything felt connected and my slightest move of any part of my body caused the other parts to react.

He rubbed his bearded jaw while looking at my body. "This looks like a good start, little one. But we are far from finished." He reached for something small behind him and began to attach nipple clamps onto my chest. The small metal torture devices were soon biting into my hard nipples. He attached small chains from the clamps to the metal ring on the middle of my chest.

"Better," he said. "Turn and grab your ankles, Servant."

I did with full knowledge of what was coming next. Master lubed a dildo and placed it against my rosebud. It felt small to me like the tip of a pencil eraser, so I was intrigued. I had just assumed that he would once again shove his largest butt plug into me, but I was wrong.

When Master finally pushed the dildo forward, I saw his devilish plan. The dildo was small in girth but was tremendously long as it snaked up into my guts. It was probably just as long as my Master's cock but felt very different since the girth was not spreading my anal ring wide. He pushed the dildo forward and then retracted it all the way out before ramming it home again.

"Very responsive, little one," he said as he worked that fake cock back and forth inside of me.

The alpha wolf must have attached the dildo to one of the chains because he soon removed his hand, but the long piece of plastic stayed in place. It felt okay now, but I knew this was going to be a real problem if he left it in me for any significant amount of time.

"Stand up straight, my Servant, and face me," he ordered. I want to make sure that you are presentable."

I did and felt the effects of each movement deep inside my body. My new Master reached around me, grabbed my ass cheeks, and pulled me between his legs. He was still seated, but now I was standing body to body in front of him. His overwhelming closeness left me unsettled, not to mention his smell, the heat of his hands on my skin, and the throbbing piece of man meat between his legs that was now pressed against my own.

He stuck out his tongue and actually licked my mark from my chin to my earlobe. I had never had anyone do that to me before and it caused cold chills to run up my spine.

"You are mine now, my Servant. I will make every decision for you so that you do not have to worry about anything. I have marked you as mine with my smell and my seed. No one will bother you and I will provide you with your every possible desire. Do you understand?"

"Yes, Master."

"Good. I'm going to feed you now and then you will hang behind me while I take care of some pack business. Afterwards, we will have a ceremony where you will be presented to the pack. You will make me very happy tonight."

I nodded my consent, even though he didn't care about it or need it. Wondering what the phrase *presented to the pack* was going to entail, I immediately got a mental image of a huge gang-bang with a large group of beautiful men.

Master picked up a plate of food from behind him on the bed and patiently started to feed it to me. Paprika potatoes and fried eggs were first. Buttered toast and fresh cantaloupe were given to me next. Each bite was washed down with strong black coffee. His intense gaze rarely left mine as he treated me like a child. In between each one of my bites, he took one as well. We both ate a lot before we were sated.

"Enough." Master stood up and ordered, "Follow me, little one. I am anxious to get this over with so that I can once again be planted firmly inside that sweet ass of yours."

I walked gingerly after him, feeling every single muscle movement reverberating deep inside of me. Master led the way into the throne room where he used a set of buttons recessed into the wall to lower a hook from the ceiling. He positioned me under the hook, attached it to the restraints holding my wrists together and then raised it once again.

Master adjusted the height of the hook several different times before he was satisfied. I went from standing flat-footed on the floor to swinging completely in the air. The final height was one in which just the tips of my toes could touch the cold stone floor so I was reaping the sensations of both being anchored and swinging free.

It didn't take me more than a few seconds to see Master's logic in this position. If I swung free, I could separate my legs slightly to offer relief from the torment of the long dildo inserted in my ass, but my cock was painfully stimulated and my arms hurt from the weight. If I put my toes down on the floor and steadied myself, the dildo felt huge in my tight hole and caused me to squeeze it hard. This gave relief to my cock and arms but tortured my nipples and ass.

"You are beautiful like this, little one."

I was sure that the strain on my face was not attractive, but I did appreciate my Master being kind to me. His icy blue eyes burned with desire and lust for me when I looked into them.

"One last thing," he said almost to himself as he disappeared into the bedroom and returned with a strip of cotton. He fed it between my lips and securely tied it onto the back of my head. Master closed the bedroom door before climbing the stairs to his chair.

The alpha wolf was in all of his naked hairy glory as he swung one massively muscled leg up onto the chair arm, exposing his crotch much like he had on the first day that I had met him. He turned his head to see me and winked.

"Bring in the petitioners." Master's voice boomed inside my head and I heard the other pack members begin to scramble to obey his directive. I tried to swing freely to relieve the pressure on my feet and ass as the grand door opened.

Several members of the pack escorted in an elderly man who was clutching his fedora in his hands. The pack members, like my Master, were easily recognized because they were freaking gorgeous with great bodies and totally naked.

I watched in fascination as the old man looked from the naked pack master to the naked Servant swinging slightly behind him and back again. He looked shocked and fascinated at the same time. He nervously made his way to the base of the stairs. His clothes were well made and looked expensive.

"Yes?" Master asked in his booming voice.

"What are you guys doing here? Running a nudist colony?"

My new Master snapped, "Do I look like I'm here to answer to you?"

"No, sir," the old man said quickly while bowing his head.

"What do you want here?"

"My name is Drovac Sadorny."

"And?"

The elderly man quickly blurted out his request. "I own a small construction company in Cluj and have come to petition you to see if I might be awarded the rights to construct the cell phone towers that your telecommunications company is going to need to build."

"Epsilon, Kappa!" Master shouted.

Two older handsome wolves scrambled forward. One of them addressed my Master with just a quick glance at me, "We received two offers for this job, one of which is from his company, sir."

The second one said, "I have reviewed the contracts, sir. Both bids are pretty close to each other." This wolf had to be a lawyer.

The older man was constantly staring at me at this point,

making me uncomfortable. I stared back at him just to show him that I was not ashamed to be hanging naked behind my Master.

"It's your decision, Alpha," the first wolf said.

"I will ask my new Servant what he thinks," my Master said, surprising me. Based on the looks on the werewolves' faces, I wasn't the only one. He turned to me and his voice appeared in my head. *"Well, little one?"*

"Alpha, I don't think it is right to have this marked man make decisions for the pack," the lawyer thought before I could think anything.

"I don't care what you think on this subject, Epsilon. If I want my new Servant to decide, it is my choice."

"Sutton?"

"What is he willing to do for us, Master?"

My Master turned back towards the petitioner and said, "My Servant, very wisely, would like to know what you are willing to do for us, Sadorny."

The older man's head swiveled back and forth between me and Master. He sputtered, "He . . . I . . . he . . . what I am willing to do?" Master nodded and there was silence as he considered the question. "What, like money?" he finally asked.

"Do we look like we need your money?" Master snapped.

"No, sorry. I don't know what you would want." He held his hands out in supplication.

"He owns a racehorse that has won many prizes, sir," the lawyer informed my Master.

The old man blanched completely white. "No! He is my prized possession."

"Little one, do we take his prized racehorse?" Master challenged me.

"We take the first two foals, Master." I felt sorry for the old man.

Master stared at me with the burning blue intensity of a

star imploding on itself. I had been trying to anchor myself to the floor during the whole time this petitioner was in the room, but now I found it impossible. I lifted my toes and spread my legs slightly to get some relief. Master smiled at my discomfort and turned back to the old man.

"Sadorny, My Servant believes that you will owe us the first two foals sired by your racehorse."

"Deal," he agreed quickly as the blood rushed into his face again.

"My men will have you sign some paperwork on your way out."

"So, I will get the contracts?"

"As long as you please me. Don't make me regret it," Master said firmly.

"No, I won't." He bowed to my Master and then turned and did the same to me.

"Next," Master said loudly, dismissing the man.

The night continued in this manner with Master sometimes asking my opinion about the different petitioners. There were a total of four cases, some quite complicated.

"Is this it?" Master thought to us after the fourth one.

"There is one more after dinner, Alpha. A Romi."

I knew this as the Romanian term for a gypsy, and I was intrigued about what one of them would be petitioning the Hounds for.

"Very well. I will need to take my Servant down and give him a hard fucking before dinner anyway."

Master's words, even in my head, were such a turn-on that I was in danger of self-immolating. My cock was already hard as a steel beam, and I didn't think I could stand much more pressure. Master was right when he said that he needed to give me a hard fucking, because I didn't think that I could go another minute without it.

Chapter Twenty-Five

Part of a written response from the Alpha of the Hounds' father delivered overnight by courier, but not read until the next morning:

Dear Son,

It is very good to hear from you, and I am thrilled to be able to try to help you with the problem that you presented to me in your letter. It also warms my heart that you do not have the answers to everything!

You are indeed lucky to have captured this individual that you wrote about. He is a very rare man indeed, if he is everything that you have said he is and has the skills that you describe.

I have never heard of a marked man who could become a wolf and I have bitten many of them in my day. Furthermore, I have never heard of a wolf who could listen into your pack talk without being a member of the pack itself. It is a very strange and perplexing situation in which you find yourself.

I consulted with my Gamma who is quite the lycan historian, if you remember, and he reminded me of a childhood story that I had not thought about for years. I will pass it onto you and see if you can make heads or tails of it.

The story, usually told by the Romi, went something like this —

Once there was a noble pack of wolves that excelled and succeeded in all areas of life. The pack master was a remarkable man known for his intellect, business acumen, and physical strength. But above all else, he was known for his cock and how to use it.

The pack master could have any man in the village to fuck and he quite frequently did, but he was not ever satisfied with them.

One day a marked man spoke to him in the way of the wolf and let him shove his big cock up his hole.

Master waited until the reception hall had cleared out before he removed me from where I was hanging and released me from the chains, cuffs, and dildo that had been tormenting me for the past three hours. He lay me down on the bed and propped my head on a pillow before shoving another one under my crotch to lift my ass up.

He lubed his cock well before sliding it home inside of me. "Fuuuuccccckkkk," he groaned as that massive pole spread me wide open and filled every conceivable inch of my insides.

I also moaned loudly into the pillow because the super-long dildo had done nothing but cause an inferno of need deep inside me that my Master was now scratching, as only he could. I pushed my ass up to meet each one of his thrusts and practiced using my ass muscles to milk his big beast as he fucked me.

My new Master poured himself into me, shooting ropy strands of man cream far into my innards. He groaned with his satisfaction and I smiled into the pillow, wondering how I got so lucky.

"It's time I put some other type of protein into you, my Servant," he informed me in his still-husky voice. "Go clean yourself, and then meet me in the reception room."

I nodded my understanding and quickly scrambled to obey as soon as he rolled off me and helped me up. I didn't think my ass was ever going to feel the same again, and I was okay with that so long as my Master continued to shower me with his attention.

I jumped into the cleaning pool and quickly washed the sweat and cum off of my skin. I tried to make sure that my ass wasn't going to leak my Master's man-goo once I was clean by doing the best scoop job I could with my fingers, but I'm afraid it didn't do much.

Drying off quickly, I walked as fast as my sore ass would allow me out to the throne room where I saw my Master talking to Epsilon, the lawyer.

Master was saying, "He's not a complete wolf."

"Then what is he?"

"I'm not sure yet, but I will find out."

I stopped at the doorway where they could see me so they wouldn't think that I was trying to listen.

"He's here," Epsilon said.

My Master turned to me. "Servant, come here."

I came to stand beside him. He affectionately grabbed my neck and ran his big hand through my hair, pulling my head close to his nose. "You are clean now and hungry, little one?"

"Yes, Master."

"Go to the dining room, Servant, sit in the chair on the end. I will be there shortly."

I nodded and turned to go.

"Alpha, I cannot protest this strongly enough," I heard the lawyer say.

"He can eat with us," Master said with an air of frustration.

I was soon out of earshot. It took me a couple of seconds to find the dining room, but the smell of food soon led me there. I opened huge French doors and saw an amazingly long table loaded with food. Every one of the men seated at the long table was a wolf—handsome and huge.

They were all talking animatedly about their night of conquests until I headed to the table, and then it went dead quiet in the room but not in my head.

"Look, it's the Alpha's marked man."

"What the fuck is he doing in here?"

"He's not a Hound. He shouldn't be here."

"*Where is the Alpha?*"

"*I'm surprised that he can even walk after the Alpha has fin-ished with him.*"

Chuckling, I had to admit that I was not walking with my normal gait. Every step reminded me that he had fucking railed me out many times with that huge cock of his. Slowly and purposefully, I made my way to the head of the table, pulled back the chair there, and sat down.

"You dare sit in the Alpha's chair?" one of the older men yelled at me.

"It's bad enough he is here at all," one of the younger men yelled from further down the table.

I raised my voice and spoke with authority. "I am here because the Alpha told me to come."

"You don't belong here."

"You are not one of us."

I swallowed hard and defiantly said, "I am now."

"Why?"

"Because your Alpha is now my Master."

"Since when?" one of them challenged me.

"Since the moment his big dick slid inside me."

"Well said, little one," a booming voice said from the doorway.

Turning to look, I saw my Master and the lawyer striding towards us. My new Master stopped and grabbed the top of my chair while the lawyer took his seat. He addressed the table of gathered Hounds.

"This is Sutton. He is now my Servant. You will accept him as one of us and show him respect from now on."

"Yes, Alpha," they all said in unison.

I should have been happy with Master's words and with the fact that the werewolves agreed to it so easily, but I felt unsettled. Something was happening. It started slowly, but there was a disquiet that I felt like a low rumbling right be-fore an earthquake. A shudder ran through me and I could have sworn that I saw the same shudder run through the pack. Master barely moved but I saw him blink his beautiful eyes several times without reason.

"Where is Theta?" Master asked suddenly, breaking the silence with the deep voice that made my balls tingle with excitement.

"He had to run an errand, Alpha," the man to my Master's left informed him. "He will return after dinner."

"Make sure of it," Master commanded. "We shall hold a ceremony for me to properly present Sutton to the pack tonight. I expect everyone's attendance."

"Yes, Alpha," they said in unison.

I was amazed that these men had no problems questioning me but were absolutely compliant with my Master's orders. There was not even a simmering thought of disobedience.

"Stand, little one," he commanded. I stood up immediately. "My Servant, this is my best friend and my Beta." He indicated the man to his left who was close to his age. Beta was very handsome—dark hair where my Master's was brown, short and stocky, with tattoo-covered muscled arms to die for. His broad chest was completely covered in dark bristly hair.

I nodded to him.

"And this is Omega, our youngest wolf," Master said indicating the young man on his right.

Omega couldn't have been more than eighteen years old. He was thin and ripped like a marathon runner with a bird chest. His long blonde hair hung in curtains over his face like a pop star. I noticed the tattoos on his neck and hands and approved of them immediately.

I nodded to him as well.

Master pushed his silverware, napkin, and wine glass forward on the big table before swiping the plates and bowls off of it with a single movement of his big arm. "Up onto the table, Servant. Your Master is going to eat his dinner off of that sweet ass of yours."

I heard the words but didn't register them. *He's going to do what?*

"Now!" he growled.

I scrambled to plank myself across the table. It was a giant table, so it easily held most of my six-feet three-inch frame with just my head and feet hanging off. Master adjusted his chair closer to Omega so that my ass was right in front of him.

He is really going to do this!

I saw the looks of wonder on the faces of the Hounds, except for the Beta. His face was one of sheer delight and lust. I could tell that he idolized my Master just from that one look.

Master clapped his hands and the doors flew open. I smelled the food before I saw it. Whoever was serving the food was doing so quickly and quietly. I thought I heard at least five people travelling around the table. Something cold was placed on my ass and then something hot. Whatever the last thing was, it had some kind of sauce with it and that was soon running down into the crack of my ass and onto the back of my balls.

One by one, the servers made their way towards the Beta's plate and then around to look at me in the face. Most of them quickly looked down, but the last one was an older man who looked like he was in his late fifties. He took one look at me and dropped the silver serving tray that he was carrying.

The tray clanged on the hardwood floors loudly and the food splattered the Alpha and the Beta's legs and feet.

"God dammit!" Master bellowed as he stood up quickly from his chair. He turned to the older man. "Pick it up."

The server's eyes had never left mine and now all he could do was shake his head from side to side violently.

"Pick it up!" Master commanded more firmly.

The server finally looked at him with horror, turned on heel, and ran out of the room.

"What the fuck is going on?" my Master asked Beta behind my head. Then he turned his icy blue eyes on me.

I felt like he could see right through me—into my brain and into my soul.

"*Well?*" Master's voice appeared inside of my head and he sounded pissed off.

"*Is he a gypsy, Master?*"

"*Yes, little one. Why?*"

"*I seem to have that effect on them, Master.*"

"*We will discuss this more after dinner, Servant. There are still things that you have not told me and that displeases me greatly.*"

"*Yes, Master.*"

Chapter Twenty-Six

One side of a phone conversation overheard outside of the kitchen at Hound Manor. The oldest server, Alin Bransas, was speaking to an unknown party:

"He's here."
"I don't know how he found it."
"By his own accord, I think."
"I didn't know it was him until I saw him at dinner."
"He has caught the Alpha's eye."
"I don't think they know."
"No, they are still unchanged."
"There is one missing."
"Yeah, that's good for us."
"What should I do?"
"I heard something about a ceremony tonight."
"With all of them, I think."
"How?"
"I don't think they will listen to me."
"I won't be able to get close enough to him to try anything. He is almost always under or beside the Alpha."
"I will have to leave if that happens."

Each food item that Master ate off of my ass he also shared with me. These wolves had tremendous appetites and I was hungry as shit as well, so Master and I ate a lot. I enjoyed licking his palm and fingers clean after he had pushed the food into my mouth each time.

The alpha wolf who was eating his dinner off my ass cheeks had forgone the use of silverware. He was eating everything with his mouth, which was driving me crazy. His beard and tongue were relentlessly tickling and stroking my sensitive skin and asshole. When I looked at him, his beard was coated in food and gravy, but he didn't seem to care. His fingers smeared the food all over my face as he made sure that they were constantly working themselves into my mouth.

From the sounds of the other wolves behind me, I assumed that they were also not eating with utensils. The dessert was apple strudel with ice cream and it wasn't long before my complete ass crack was coated in melted cream.

"Your hot little asshole keeps melting my ice cream, Servant," Master growled at me as he shoved another bite of strudel coated in ice cream into my mouth.

I didn't speak, but I apologized with my eyes. His beautiful blue eyes rarely left mine which at once warmed my heart, titillated my balls, and unnerved me.

"Enough," Master's voice boomed in the great room. "I expect you all in the reception room in an hour. I'm going to clean my Servant, see the last petitioner, and then we will be ready to start the ceremony."

Master reached down and rolled me over, knocking over glasses and plates in my path. His thick arms snaked under my knees and shoulders as he pulled me to him. Easily lifting me off the table, the alpha wolf carried me out of the room to his bathroom and straight into the cleaning pool.

My new Master quickly washed me, concentrating on making my ass pink and shiny. No words were said until I was clean and dry. "You will be strapped to a cross beside me for the last petitioner, my Servant. I do not have time to properly restrain you, so this will have to do."

"Yes, Master."

"After this petitioner, we will have a short break to pre-pare you for the ceremony. I would like to hear about your experiences with the Romi at that time. Do you understand, Servant?"

"Yes, Master." *I hope that he's not mad at me or thinks that I was withholding information from him.*

"Come," he ordered. I hastened after him to the throne room.

Master lowered a huge wooden structure in the shape of the letter X down from the ceiling and strapped my wrists to it. He slipped a ball gag over my head and made sure the rubber bit was between my teeth.

"Raise your legs, my Servant," he commanded huskily.

I pulled on my wrist straps and swung my legs into the air. Master greased up a butt plug and firmly shoved it into me. He strapped it in place with elastic bands around my upper thighs that held it firmly planted inside me.

"Very good, Sutton," he said to me as he strapped my an-kles down to the cross. My backside against the wooden cross caused the butt plug to grind into me which produced a myriad of sensations in my brain. I liked it when he called me by my name, but I also wondered if it meant that he would eventually soften in his domination of me. I didn't want that to happen.

Master took his seat beside me on his throne and called telepathically for the last petitioner of the day.

Soon, the heavy doors flew open and several naked wolves entered with a young man who kept his head bowed the entire time. I noticed with regret that his clothing looked like those worn by some of the gypsies that I had encoun-tered while I had been in Romania. I had forgotten that Master had said that he would be a Gypsy.

"Come forward," Master called to him.

The young man moved steadily forward without looking

up. I wondered immediately if he was bowing his head as a sign of respect or hiding something about himself. When he got to the base of the steps leading up to Master's chair, he knelt on the hardwood floors.

"What do you want?" Master asked in his booming voice.

The young Gypsy looked up at my Master and said, "I am Lin Pastrovia, Excellency and I . . ." He trailed off suddenly as he saw me. Turning his head towards me, the blood rushed out of his face.

"*Catalizator*," he mouthed to me, but no sound came from his lips. What did come from his lips next was a giant loogie of spit which he flung at me. It hit me on the leg.

Master must have jumped from his chair to the space in front of the young Gypsy, because he seemed to appear out of nowhere. He immediately grabbed the man by the throat and lifted him off his knees.

"You will not!" Master growled at him.

The young man made some sort of strangled noise and I wondered if my new Master was going to kill him. Instead, he got his angry face right in front of the Romi's and asked, "Why did you spit on my Servant?" His voice was commanding and forceful.

The young man did not want to answer, but my Master was not to be denied the information that he contained. The alpha werewolf tightened his grip on the man's throat until the Gypsy's eyes were bugging out of his face. "Are you ready to tell me?"

The man nodded with his purple face.

My new Master relaxed his grip on the man's neck and the young Romi began to sputter and cough. "Well?" Master asked showing no signs of sympathy for the young man's plight.

"He is the *Catalizator*," the man finally squeaked out between his clenched teeth.

"The *Catalizator*?" Master asked looking at me with curiosity coloring his face.

I shrugged my shoulders in response.

"Why do you call him that?" Master demanded as he lowered his face to the young Romi's.

"Because that is what he is."

"What does it mean?" Master growled through barred teeth.

"I don't know."

Master made a show of balling his big fist in front of the frightened kid's face.

"The elders know but do not tell us. They warned that he was coming and then again that he was here."

"Get out!" Master yelled at the gathered crowd, while never taking his eyes off of me.

"But what about my . . ." the young Gypsy began.

"You are done. I don't give a shit about what you want," the Alpha snapped to the petitioner. "Get him the hell out of here," he commanded the members of his pack that were present. He used pack talk to tell the wolves that he wanted them to set up for the ceremony.

Master began to unstrap me from the cross before the man was carried kicking and screaming out of the hall. He released my gag. "Bathroom, Sutton."

I rubbed my wrists as I hurried to my Master's bathroom. The alpha wolf followed right behind me, closing the door behind him. He sat down on a bench on the side of the bathroom and reached into a recessed cabinet. He pulled out a jar and a paint brush.

"Stand here, my Servant." He pointed at the slate floor in front of him.

I hastened to follow his command.

Master's icy blue eyes held me in their gaze. I knew that I would be unable to tell him anything but the truth. "The word that he called you, Servant. Do you know what it means?"

"I was told that it means catalyst, Master," I admitted.

"But you don't know why they call you that?"

"No, Master."

"Have you heard it before?"

"Yes, Master." I could see in his eyes that he wanted me to continue, so I did. "Almost every Gypsy that I have encountered since I came to Romania has yelled that at me, especially the older ones, Master."

"Do you know why?"

"I do not, Master."

He looked at me curiously and said, "Why would they call you catalyst?"

"Do you think that is the word for what I am, Master?" I asked. *Why would they yell that at me? What does all this even mean?*

"Does that word mean anything to you, Sutton?"

"No, Master."

"Very well. Yet another part of the puzzle that I have to figure out about you, little one."

"If I knew, I would tell you, Master," I said with sincerity.

"You better," he growled.

Master took the lid off the jar, dipped the brush inside, and pulled it out. I saw that the brush looked like it had gold paint on it. The alpha Hound touched the wet brush to my hip and began to paint me. His free hand was used to spin me slowly as he worked.

"This will show the pack what your assets are," Master said softly. "This ceremony is not meant to demean you, Sutton, but to highlight you."

"Yes, Master."

He continued to paint my ass cheeks until he finished on the other hip. He moved up to my face and painted swatches of color on my cheeks and around my mouth. Master finished by coating my hands in gold.

"You will be fantastic," he said with pride in his tone. "I will be right back, my Servant. Stand here and dry," he ordered me as he put away the jar and brush before leaving the room.

Master returned carrying a long strip of leather with a collar on one end. I looked at it questioningly.

"You want to ask your Master something?" he asked.

"Yes, Master."

"You may."

"You told me that your pack had never had a marked man before and that you had not ever heard of a marked man being a werewolf before."

"Yes."

"Then what is this ceremony that you are preparing me for?"

He looked at me with a tilt to his head. "Do you mean to ask how is it that we have a ceremony for something that has never happened before?"

"Yes, Master."

"I am modifying the ceremony that we use when we add a new pack member to make it special for you, Sutton. Because you are my special one, right?"

"Yes, Master," I said with a flush of my painted skin and a grin.

"Good. Now, what will happen is that the pack will gather. You and I will be in the center of the circle and I will announce you as a new member. I will mark you as ours and then you will be one of us. Do you understand?"

"Yes, Master." I suddenly felt a very strange pull to the other room. It was unsettling, like the insistent tug of a strong undertow at the beach. I was being drawn to the throne room.

The alpha werewolf didn't say anything more but chose

to strap the studded collar around my neck. The very long leather cording draped down my back. When he was finished, he stood back to admire his work.

"I've never seen you so nervous before, Sutton," he commented. "Not when we captured you, not when we paraded you through the house, not when you were hung behind me for the petitioners to see, not when I ate off of your ass, or when you were negotiating with me at our first meeting. What is wrong?"

Before I could answer him and tell him about the draw that I was experiencing, the door to that room opened. "We are ready, Alpha," a voice from the door announced.

"Very good," Master said loudly. "It is time," he said softly to me as he grabbed the leather leash hooked to my collar and pulled me after him as he headed for the throne room.

I felt like I was falling. The pull of whatever was in the throne room had me under its power and Master was walking towards it quickly, so I was on a collision course with something unexplainable. The urge to go to the throne room increased with each step until my heart was pounding and the blood was rushing in my ears.

Something was happening to me, but I had no idea what it was. But whatever it was, my new Master and I were about to slam headlong into it.

CHAPTER TWENTY-SEVEN

Excerpt of a passage in the History of the Hell Hounds titled *How We Lost the Ability to Completely Change:*

Werewolves were scarce and scattered across the globe in the early days of the world. With the dawn of the Industrial Revolution, people began to move to the cities, which drew many wolfpacks to join their ranks.

Deaths, especially by wild animals, were harder to explain in the cities and many wolves were discovered or revealed to be mass murders. Disputes were more likely to be handled in a court of law or by the police now rather than being settled between the two offended parties. The growing availability of trains allowed wolves to expand their territories and many packs' memberships swelled to outrageous numbers.

All of these factors spelled trouble for werewolves. We desperately wanted to go undiscovered but the larger packs took a toll on the local resources and the media sensationalized any of our kills. A change had to occur to ensure the survival of our kind.

In the year eighteen forty-two, the Lycan Council declared that packs may only expand to twenty-two members – the same number of letters in the Greek alphabet. They also banned werewolves from completely changing to wolf form in the cities, punishable by death.

The council was very concerned that if a werewolf was discovered by the police that there would be a purge on their species like they had never experienced before. With few exceptions, the wolves did as the council ordered and after fifty years without tasting flesh, all werewolves began to lose their ability to make the second change during the full moon.

I followed my Master into the reception room to prepare for the ceremony that would mark me as one of the Hounds. I wasn't sure what was about to happen, but I couldn't even think about it, because I was having some kind of physical reaction to the gathering of the pack.

Sweating profusely already, my mind flooded with thoughts as I entered the room. All of the Hounds were assembled and formed a solemn circle in the middle of the room. They were all kneeling on one knee and were surrounded by lit torches in sconces on the walls. The other lights in the room had been extinguished. The gold paint on my body looked like shimmering smoke as it reflected the firelight.

The wolves were nervous—I could feel the energy in the room and, of course, I could hear their thoughts. They were reading the nervous energy as a sign that I should not be made a member of the pack. I was hoping that there was another cause for it, but I had no clue what that would be. It was amazing to see such an assembled group of handsome men, all of their beautiful dicks hard and pointed to the sky.

"All right, my Servant?" Master asked me firmly as he grabbed me by the nape of my neck and squeezed. The smell of fresh pineapple and new tennis balls was overwhelming me. It was his smell, and I hoped to be able to smell it every day from here on out.

"Master, they don't want me."

He looked at me with such passion that I blushed immediately. "They don't know what is good for them, Sutton. It is my job to do what is best for the pack—what is good for them, whether they recognize it or not."

"How are you so confident that I am what is best for the pack, Master?"

"Because I am your Master, little one. And because I am their Alpha. Say it," he ordered.

"You are my Master, Master." I winked to let him know that I was being funny.

"Don't get smart with me, little one. I will punish you right here in the middle of the circle in front of my pack."

"Sorry, Master," I said quickly.

He regarded me seriously for a second. "Don't you trust me?"

"I do, Master."

"Then let's do this."

It had not escaped my notice that in the middle of the circle was Master's foam pad. There was no doubt that I was about to get my world rocked right here in front of all these wolves. I was perfectly fine with that, but I didn't want whatever it was that had me so out-of-sorts to interfere with my time with my Master.

I walked confidently into the middle of the circle and waited for my Master to catch up with me. The thoughts from the wolves were buzzing in my head just like I had stepped into the middle of a beehive. I had never been so overstimulated with activity in my head before. Taking a deep breath, my sinus cavity was flooded with the smell of musky testosterone. Every man in this room was emitting a wave of sexual pheromones that was making my head swim.

"On all fours, Servant," Master's deep voice cut through the din of the buzzing.

I bent over and lowered myself to my knees onto the middle of the foam pad. I could feel all of the eyes on me as well as see them shining at me in the torchlight. My Master stepped towards me and ran the long length of leather that had been hanging down my back around my hips. I didn't see the logic to what he was doing until a few seconds later.

When I tried to lower my head, the dog collar wouldn't

let me. It was attached to my waist which kept it from stray-
ing too far from where it was. Master completed my bondage by attaching a thinner strip of leather around my forehead and pulling it way back before attaching the leather
thong to the one running down my back.

My head was now stretched painfully back and my
mouth was stretched wide open as it was pointed up at the
ceiling. Master walked around me, studying his work. He
kept a hot hand on me as he circumnavigated my awkwardly positioned body. His tremendous cock was rock-hard and
pointing up and out as he walked.

"Your mouth must be open and pointed skyward, my
Servant," he whispered to me. I was reassured that this was
part of the ceremony and not just something that he was doing to make me feel pain. My brain drew a mental picture of
the position and I immediately recognized it as the classic
silhouette of the wolf howling at the moon.

Master turned away from me and addressed his pack.
"My brothers, tonight is a very special event. I can feel your
excitement and smell the musky odor of your anticipation."

The alpha wolf paused for dramatic reasons as he began
to circle me, facing outward to his pack members. "Tonight,
we induct a new member into our ranks. Not just any member, but a different kind of brother. This is Sutton. He is my
Servant and will be accepted by my pack."

"Show him," Master commanded with a growl.

"Sutton, brother," the collected men said in unison, heads
still bowed.

"Let us celebrate our good fortune for finding this Servant
and having him accept us for what we are. I will now complete the ceremony. You may watch Sutton's transcendence
to our pack, my wolves."

The alpha wolf knelt behind me and greased his big rod. I
couldn't wait for it to be inside of me. When Master was

ready, he placed his over-sized cock head against my puckered hole and paused.

Master's deep voice boomed out in the quiet room, "I mark Sutton as a Hound of Hell." I was still thinking about his statement when the Alpha slammed his hips forward and penetrated me as completely as anyone ever had.

It almost knocked me off of my hands and knees. My new Master's thrust had been so deep and so hard that it had propelled me forward. Only his strong hands on my hips holding me back kept me from falling flat on my exposed neck.

Master never let go of my hips, using them to meet each one of his powerful thrusts forward. Sweat poured down both of our bodies and his palms on my skin felt like branding irons. His cock was the true brand—burning my asshole and marking my anal channel as belonging to him.

I was having trouble thinking straight, but I was pretty sure that I had never been fucked like this before. It was glorious and exciting to think that this was only the beginning of my time with my Master.

It didn't bother me in the least that he was railing me out in front of a crowd. I could hear the others' thoughts and they were just as impressed as I was by Master's dominance over me. Feeling that Master was reaching his climax, I could feel my own at the same time—a slow ache deep in my balls that was building.

The alpha wolf picked up his pace—fucking faster, deeper, and more aggressively. Master and I were both grunting and groaning as we headed like a brakeless train towards the depot. I could feel my climax moving up from my balls towards my chest. I bucked and fought against the leather straps holding my head back.

"Master," I groaned hoarsely. I could just barely make out the word due to the awkward position of my mouth.

"Servant," he returned with an equal tone.

We were seconds away from our climax. I could feel my Master's release coming just as easily as I could feel mine. My climax was building so fast and so completely that it felt like my insides were going to explode out of my prick.

Slowly, my release moved up my cock—from the base, to the middle of the shaft, to the cock head. My heart was beating so fast and I think I had stopped breathing altogether.

The dam burst dramatically. The cum vent on my prick opened and I shot a powerful strand of hot spunk onto the foam pad under me. Master also roared with his release.

Something else began to emerge from deep in my nuts. It came fast and hard while I was still shooting cum. A massive howl came out of my lungs before I even knew what was happening. Master immediately joined me with a deep-throated howl of his own. All of the wolves were soon howling along with us.

I was exhausted, but there was still something else. I could feel it just like Master's cock still throbbing inside me. Impulsively, I yelled, "Bite me, Master!"

The alpha wolf stopped in mid-thrust. In confusion, he asked, "What?"

I knew it was hard for him to understand me with my mouth pulled wide open, so I repeated it at the top of my lungs. "Bite me, Master!" I also thought it for good measure.

Master roared again before hunching over me and biting me on the shoulder. Pain, like a red lightning bolt, hit me with the full force of Zeus throwing it down from the heavens. I thought I might pass out from it, but somehow I maintained my position.

Blood dripped from Master's mouth onto my back. It felt like he had taken a chunk of my skin with him when he bit me. Suddenly, my head was free and I painfully lowered it before feeling sharp pains on my hips where Master's hands were resting.

My head exploded with thoughts from the other wolves causing my head to snap up to see what the commotion was about. Looking around the circle, I saw the look of awe on each one of the Hounds' faces. Most of them were slack-jawed as they stared over my shoulder.

Is it blood lust? Are the other wolves jealous of my Master for what he had? I could see the lust in their eyes and the heady smell of testosterone permeated the room. Master's cum was deep in my ass and his smell was deep in my sinus cavities.

I turned to look at my Master, who was still planted firm-ly inside me. My neck only twisted around enough to see his hand on my hip. But where his hand should have been, there was now a paw with long black nails that were digging into my flesh. The paw was covered with my Master's glorious golden-brown hair.

CHAPTER TWENTY-EIGHT

Part of the official criteria to become a werewolf as written in the Hounds of Hell charter.

Men shall not be made werewolf unless –
The pack has less than twenty-0..0two members
The pack can sustain another member, both financially and emotionally
The community is stable
One has gained approval of the Alpha
The man has been vetted and meets the criteria set below

Men selected to be made werewolf have to meet the following criteria –
At least eighteen years of age
Have chosen this life
Have never committed a murder
No history of mental illness
No sons at the time of the turn
Approval by the entire pack
Are non-marked
Are athletic
Are respectable members of society
Have an established job

My Master let out a roar that let me know that he was no longer human just as I twisted my head violently to see him. The alpha wolf was literally a wolf now—a gorgeous golden-brown wolf that was on his haunches with his front paws on my sides and his dick still planted deep inside me.

"Master?"

"Servant, are you frightened of me?"

"No, Master."

"Good, because you have done this to me."

"Is this why they call me the Catalyst, Master?"

"It must be, little one."

The pack talk between Master and me was interrupted by another blood-curdling howl. We both looked forward to see Boris changing into a wolf as well. He turned into a very black, slightly smaller version of the Alpha. My eyes couldn't focus on Boris for long, because to my right, came another very loud howl.

Ianu was also changing. His form morphed into that of a large grey wolf within seconds. He shook his shaggy head at me and his dark eyes penetrated my very soul.

"Well fuck me," I said under my breath as I watched in amazement.

"That's what it is, little one. Fucking you is the key to us changing."

I hadn't put the pieces together yet, but Master had. The thoughts from the other wolves soon overwhelmed me.

"How are you doing that, Alpha?"

"Look how bad-ass they look."

"I'm trying, but I can't change."

"You have to have fucked Master's Servant."

"Lucky ass!"

"Really lucky ass, if he can make us completely change!"

"I'm next in line to fuck him then!"

"Not if I get to him first."

"I'm going to rip his ass apart!"

"Enough!" My Master roared inside our heads as he pulled his big wolf dick out of me and quickly padded around the inside of the circle. I collapsed onto the foam pad without ever taking my gaze off of my amazing Master. I could swear that I could see Master's beautiful sleeves of tattoos running up the wolf's hairy front legs.

He continued with a bellowing roar inside our heads. *"No one is to ever disrespect my Servant. Do you understand?"*

"Yes, Alpha."

"It seems to be true that now that I have bitten my little one, if you have fucked him, you can take the next step and turn completely."

"Let us fuck him, Alpha."

"No!" Master roared so loudly that he suddenly transferred back into the huge shape of my handsome Master. He looked at me with such want and need that it made my heart hurt. He turned back to address his pack, saying, "I will make sure that each one of you have . . . a little bit of time with my new Servant in the coming three weeks. That way, at the next full moon, our pack will be completely able to turn."

A cheer went up from the Hounds and the two that were in wolf form howled instead. Some of the men in the circle began to jack their cocks.

"Now, I am going to show my new Servant how extremely happy I am with him and then Ianu, Boris, and I are going to go into the woods on a hunt just like our ancestors did centuries ago!"

Another cheer went up from the crowd.

"Until then brothers, take your lust out on the men who need to be punished!"

Another cheer was given.

"Little one, to my bed," my Master ordered gruffly.

"Yes, Master," I said in anticipation of what was to come. I could barely walk from the savage fucking that the alpha werewolf had just given me before he changed, but I found my way gingerly to his bed.

Is this really happening? I had just assumed that my new

199

Master and his friends were playing at being werewolves, but here they were in the hairy flesh to prove it. I was amazed, but as shocked as I was to witness this miracle, I could think of nothing except for the fuck that my Master was going to give me in this moment.

Master strode into the room like a king but didn't stop to address me or even look at me. His long strides took him into the bathroom and then back out again. He approached me with a clean towel and a jar of ointment.

We were alone for the first time in a long time. Master stared down at me. When he spoke, his face betrayed no emotion at all. "You turned out to be very special after all, little one."

"I didn't know that would happen, Master," I said quickly by way of an apology.

"Why then did you demand for me to bite you, Sutton?"

I hung my head in shame and admitted, "I'm not sure, Master. I just felt it . . . like an urge."

The alpha wolf reached down and lifted my chin until my green eyes were pointed directly at his icy blue ones. "I can't believe that you asked me to bite you, Sutton." His lips turned up slightly at the ends.

I blushed to my very core. "I quite enjoyed it, Master."

"Yes, I noticed, little one," he smirked. "You are an amazingly brave man."

I wanted to say something to him, but I was afraid.

As if he could read my mind, my Master commanded, "Tell me."

"I think I am supposed to be with you, Master."

He laughed and agreed, "We obviously have some type of connection, little one. I don't know how you found me, but I am the luckiest wolf alive. Your place with me is assured, my Servant. As if I didn't already want to keep you because of your amazing ass and mouth, now you have this . . ."

"I feel truly lucky also to have found you, my Master." I didn't blush this time but held his gaze. My balls tingled and my cock hardened instantly.

"Don't worry. I'm going to give you what you need. But first, let me see your bite, little one."

I twisted to the side so that the alpha wolf could see my back. His warm hands were on me, further lighting my fire. His fingertips touched the bite and ran over it with surprisingly little pain.

"Is it awful, Master?" I asked with trepidation.

"It is already partially healed, little one," he answered with no inflection.

"It is, Master?" I asked in shock.

"You must have your own special ability to heal," he guessed as he rubbed the bite mark with the clean towel. "It's not surprising. We turn completely and you turn in a different way."

I had never even considered what he was saying before. "What do you mean, Master?"

He applied some of the anti-bacterial ointment to the wound before answering me. "Have you ever felt different on the days of the full moon, Sutton?"

"Yes, Master. Some days I have an easier time taking a big dick than others."

"Like yesterday, for example?" he asked, obviously remembering how I was able to take his huge cock on the first try.

"Yes, Master. I knew that I was going to be able to impale myself on your big joint."

"How?"

"I don't know. It was just a feeling that I had, Master."

He put his hand on the side of my face and slowly ran his oversized thumb across my cheek. "You change in your own way, little one."

I nodded, but not so much that he would have to remove his hand from my face.

"I'm going to fuck you so hard now," he announced in a deep husky voice.

"Yes, Master." I flushed once again.

"You didn't get hurt when I transformed, did you?"

"No, Master. That big-ass wolf cock was the same exact size as yours," I quipped.

Master growled at me in response as he pushed my back onto the bed, lifted my legs, and pulled my ass to the edge. Thankfully, there was enough cum already inside me to lube his way.

I planted my feet flat on his broad chest while the alpha wolf placed his cock head on my puckered hole. Master pushed his huge thigh muscles forward, driving that glorious joint of his straight into me. My anal ring parted like the Red Sea as his terrible serpent parted the waters.

My eyes rolled back into my head and the only sound that came out of my mouth was a mournful groan from somewhere deep inside me. Master kept pushing until his cock was buried to the hilt. I could feel the small hairs of his crotch tickling my ass cheeks.

The man I needed now more than any other I had ever encountered hunched over me and began to drive himself into and out of me over and over. His speed and the raw sense of power that he fucked with was incredible and would give anyone pause who saw it.

But when Alpha picked me up and fucked my six-feet three-inch body while he stood straight up and down, even I was impressed. His cock felt like it was reaching places inside me that not even he had conquered before.

Moving forward, Master planted my back against the wall and worked his hips to punch into me repeatedly. It was an amazing display of power and dominance and I came almost immediately. His furry belly stroked the underside of my hard cock just as effectively as a velvet glove hand job. I was soon spurting strands of hot jizz between our sweaty bodies.

"There it is, little one. Your super-tight hole is a thing of beauty."

"And only my Master knows what to do with it," I moaned.

"That's right," he hissed between clenched teeth as he flooded my anal passages with his hot seed. I could tell that Master had gone to another place after his release, but he continued to drive into me as he climaxed, as if by rote muscle memory.

I lazily ran my hand through his wet hair and down his bearded jawline. My thumb stopped on his bottom lip and pulled it down slightly. I was about to say something when I heard the bedroom door open to my right.

We both turned and saw Beta enter. He stopped in his tracks when he saw us — me still pinned to the wall and Master breathing heavily.

"Pardon me, Alpha, but someone is here to see you."

"And why didn't you just tell me in my head?" the alpha wolf snapped.

"I didn't want him to hear, Alpha." The second-in-command bowed his head.

"My brother is here?" Master asked in shock.

"Yes, Alpha."

"What the fuck does he want?"

"I don't know, but he looks like he has seen a ghost," Beta said with a raised eyebrow.

CHAPTER TWENTY-NINE

Part of an email from Sutton Pike to his two best friends in the United States sent the next day:

To: Justin, Adam
From: Sutton Pike
Re: Good news!

Hey guys,
Sorry I haven't been in touch recently, but things have been happening very quickly here. I have met the man of my dreams – my true Master. He is everything that I dreamed a man could be and he seems to like me just as much as I like him.

I know it has only been a few days since I have known him, but I know in my heart that he is the man for me. I hate to admit it, but I seem to have already fallen in love with this man. I thought it the minute I met him and knew it the second he fucked me.

I'm writing to let you guys know that I will be staying in Romania with my new Master. I loved that you two began this journey with me and will always remember your involvement that led me to him.

Of course, I want you both to come back and visit as soon as you can. My Master has a lot of very handsome, very endowed friends and I'm positive you would find them very . . . entertaining.

I had not even known that my Master had a brother and now I was about to meet him. *He's obviously a werewolf, but why isn't he in the pack? Does my new Master have any other brothers or a father that I could possibly meet? Why isn't Master happy to see him?*

My Master lowered me to the floor and said, "Get clean, little one. You will be presented to my sibling shortly."

"Yes, Master." I ran to the bathroom and scrubbed the sweat and cum off me. I soon smelled and looked clean, so I rejoined my Master in the bedroom.

He wasn't there, so I cautiously walked through to the throne room expecting to see Master talking to his brother. Instead, Master was sitting on his chair speaking softly with Beta.

"Ah, my Servant. Come to me," Master said loudly enough for me to hear.

I padded across the cavernous reception room and up the stairs to the man that I wanted to please more than any other that I had ever met.

"I want you mounted right here on my big cock where you belong, little one," Master growled at me.

I took one look at Master's cock and saw that it was harder and more intimidating than ever. Swallowing hard, I nodded my head to show my understanding. I reached for a tube of lube that was beside the chair and squirted some into my palm.

Master continued to talk with his second-in-command as I knelt in front of his chair. Smearing the lube between both my palms, I began to work over his giant pole. The heat poured off his cock while my hot hands added even more to the mix. I loved his cock and I studied it like a prized possession as I stroked it—the big beautiful head, the strong shaft that got bigger as it snaked down to his crotch, and the prominent bulging veins that promised me endless moments of ecstasy in just a short minute.

"I think it is sufficiently lubed, Servant."

Master's deep voice brought me out of my trance. I

looked up into his icy blue eyes and saw that he was smirking at me. "Sorry, Master."

"Up on my lap, little one," he said to me. Turning to Beta, he ordered, "Send him in."

"Yes, Alpha."

I stood up and Master motioned for me to turn around, facing away from him. Twisting around, I backed into him and felt his hot hands easily lift me into the air above his crotch.

"Feet on the arms, little one," he ordered me in his husky voice that drove me out of my mind.

I placed my feet on the arms of his chair, and he held his cock up to my hole. His warm hands on my hips urged me down. Master's cockhead pushed against my asshole, making it invert inside me before it finally forced open my anal ring. His soft cockhead easily slid into me. My asshole squeezed his hard shaft as it continued to penetrate me.

Realizing that I was holding my breath, I exhaled a big breath as I plunged myself further down on his huge schlong. He felt longer and wider than ever, but I was still able to completely take him.

"Damn! You are an impressive man, Sutton," he growled as he felt my ass grind against his pubic hairs.

"You also, Master."

"I want your legs up and over the arms of the chair so that my brother has a clear view of you sitting on the root of my big cock, little one. I want there to be no doubt about your abilities and that you belong to me."

"Yes, Master," I answered him as I followed his direction.

Master made sure I was firmly planted on him by lifting me slightly off of his lap and then slamming back inside me again. When he was satisfied with my position, he leaned my upper torso over to the side and held me in place. I heard the doors open at the far end of the room.

Beta entered with a big man by his side. I could smell him almost as soon as he walked through the door.

"Mr. Ambassador," my Master's deep voice boomed across the room.

"Gray," I whispered before I even realized what I was saying.

"Peakes, what the hell is happening?" Gray's deep voice filled the big space as he confidently strode towards us. "And why did I have to wait so long . . ."

Gray's voice trailed off as he made eye contact with me and I saw the dawning realization cross his face.

"Is your sense of smell so repressed that you could not smell him from the door, brother? He certainly smelled you."

"Sutton? What are you doing here?" Gray finally asked me when he was able to recover himself.

"Your brother is my new Master," I told him.

"Are you doing this to hurt me?" he asked, but I was unsure of whether he was asking me or his brother.

Master snapped, "He didn't even know we were related until you walked in here, Gray."

"But you did, Master?" I turned to look up into his beautiful blue eyes.

"It wasn't hard to find out once I met you," Master shrugged.

I turned to Gray "I told you that there was something here that I was being drawn to, Gray. It just so happened that it turned out to be your brother. I didn't want to hurt you any more than you wanted to hurt me. It is just the way it turned out."

There was an uncomfortable silence while the four of us considered what had just happened. Beta looked just as shocked as Gray and me.

"Why are you here, Gray?" Master finally asked his

sibling.

"Something happened to me tonight, Peakes, and now I am wondering if this is not a coincidence."

"Did you turn completely?" my new Master asked like he was checking to see if he remembered to bring the milk home.

"Yes. Did you also?"

"I did, as well as each of the members of my pack that had fucked Sutton here."

"What?" Gray was back to being shocked again.

Master stared at his brother while he lifted me halfway off of his huge cock and then forcibly pulled me back down. It made my eyes roll back in my head as my brain was flooded with pleasurable sensations.

"Sutton here is what the Romi call the Catalyst," the alpha wolf told his brother. "If you fuck him, you regain the ability to change completely."

"But I fucked him first months ago," Gray said in confusion.

"As far as I can tell, it didn't happen until I bit him tonight."

"You fucking bit him?" Grey asked loudly.

"I asked him to." My cock throbbed at my remembrance of the event just a little while ago.

"He demanded it," Master corrected me.

"As soon as I turned and saw my pack members follow suit, I wondered if you had also," Peakes admitted to his brother.

"A little warning would have been nice," Gray said sarcastically.

My Master answered him in the same tone, "I didn't know. Sutton didn't know. And it's the middle of the night, so you probably weren't in some kind of high-level cabinet meeting or anything, right?"

"It scared the fuck out of my Servant," Gray said sheepishly. The ends of his lips turned up into a smile.

Master chuckled and said, "You should have seen the look on Sutton's face. I was fucking him when I changed."

"Did you know something was going to happen?" Gray asked his brother.

"No."

"Did you?" he asked me.

"No."

"Why then did you want my brother to bite you?"

"It was just something I felt needed to happen." I shrugged.

Gray looked at me thoughtfully for a moment. "The same kind of feeling that you had about him?" He nodded his head at my Master.

I took one quick look into my Master's icy blue eyes and answered, "Exactly."

"Would you like to run with my wolves tonight, Gray?" my Master asked his brother.

"You're going to go hunting?" he asked, wide-eyed.

"We are. I'm going to drop another load of Carron seed deep inside Sutton and then we can get going."

"*May I be allowed to ask you and your brother some questions, Master?*"

"You can speak Pack Talk?" Gray asked with his jaw dropping.

"He has many talents," Master said with pride. He fucked into me from below several times to get my attention. "What would you like to ask us, little one?"

"Is Gray a member of the Hounds, Master?"

Peakes looked at his brother, who answered my question. "I used to be, when I first turned old enough to join. Our father was the alpha of the Hounds and I thought that would be my destiny."

"Our father got the chance to lead a pack in the United

States so he left with Gray in tow," my Master informed me.

"I chose to go," Gray said quickly.

"Our family had a lot of holdings in the U.S. We had been to visit many times and both of us had gone to school there," Peakes explained to me.

"We do like our Americans," Gray smirked.

"I love being in an American," Master said lustfully into my ear.

"I guess any old American hole will do," I replied smartly back.

"Don't test me, Sutton. I will pull you off my cock and punish you right here in front of your former lover. You know that I will and you also know your hole is the special one for me," he growled.

That's all I needed to hear.

"I decided to leave the Hounds and follow Father to America," Gray admitted.

"And you joined his pack?" I asked thinking that I had it now.

"Once you leave a pack, you may not join another," Peakes explained. "You have to become a lone wolf."

"But . . ."

Master heard my argument just as clearly as if he was inside my head and cut me off with the answer, "Except for an alpha who can go from one pack to the next, if invited."

Gray shrugged and said, "I found my way in politics instead."

I nodded.

"More questions, little one?" Master asked me softly.

"Just one, Master."

"You may ask it now."

"Why did Gray not know that I was the Catalyst? I mean, he could've told that I ran hot. And why didn't the buzzing turn into voices after he fucked me here in Romania?" Now, that I was asking questions, they were just tumbling out of my mouth.

"That is more than one question, Sutton," Master smirked. "Do you need me to finish this fuck so that you can think straight again?"

"No, I mean, yes . . ." I said, starting to get flustered.

"I guess we don't have the answers to everything yet," Gray said in defense of himself.

"Anything else before I fuck you senseless, little one?" Master growled.

"Mind if I turn your Beta while you are out hunting, Master?"

"I would like that," he said excitedly. He turned to his number two and asked, "Would you like to sample my Servant, Beta?"

"I am not worthy of your special one, Alpha," the second in command immediately said.

"He has been a loyal friend to you, Master," I said.

"How do you know that, special one?"

"I can see things, my Master."

Peakes chuckled and asked, "You are having visions now, little one?"

"It helps to have your big stick of truth buried deep inside me, Master."

"I bet it does." Master turned his head to the two big men in front of him. "Then it is settled. My Servant needs a good hard fuck which I am more than willing to give him. Then my brother and I will hunt and Beta will fuck the shit out of Sutton while we are gone. I will leave him in your protection, Beta."

Beta was suddenly alarmed. "Are you fearful of an attack, Alpha?"

"I'm not sure the pack would hurt Sutton, but if they decided to ignore my directives to wait and gain the ability to turn now, there might be a problem," he explained. "And I am suspicious of what the Romi are up to . . ."

Beta nodded his head. "I will guard him well, Alpha."

"You fucking better," Master growled and there was no way that anyone would disobey him.

Peakes Carron used his massive hands and muscles to twist me around on his big cock until I was facing him. He held onto me as he stood up with me making an impossible task look easy. He started down the stairs in front of his throne.

I wrapped both of my arms around his thick neck and lay my head down on his collarbone. Breathing in deeply of my Master's smell, I thanked the lucky stars above that he was mine and that we were connected in so many ways—cock to ass, werewolf to Catalyst, Master to Servant.

"I will be back to hunt in ten minutes. Make sure Ianu and Boris are ready," he demanded.

"Ten minutes, Master?"

"Not enough time with my dick inside you, special one?"

"There's never enough of that time, Master . . ."

"Make it an hour," he yelled back to the werewolves as he carried me into his bedroom and slammed the door shut behind us.

I put my lips onto Master's ear and whispered, "I am yours, Master."

"You are mine," he said deeply.

"Completely," I said.

The big man gently lay me down on his bed, still connected to me by his cock. He tented himself above me as I lifted my legs onto his hips and locked them in place around him.

"You and I are connected on every level, Sutton. You will lie underneath me just like this for the rest of my life."

It was the exact thing that I needed him to say. Any worry that he would have no use for me after I turned his entire pack was gone from my head. I was completely happy.

"You are satisfied with my answer, little one?" he smirked from above me.

"Yes, Master, completely satisfied."

He laughed. "I know you well enough to know that you are never completely satisfied, my Servant." He pulled his cock out of me and then punched it back inside to accentuate his point.

"Well, you will just have to keep trying, my Master."

"That is my plan," he growled as he began to fuck me with purpose.

Mine also . . .

You may also enjoy the following from eXtasy Books Inc:

The Dark Master
Crawford Rhine

Excerpt

From the journal of Grayson Edwards—June 15, 2015, at Bucharest, Romania.

Romania is turning out to be quite the treat. I slept really soundly last night after getting hammered by Nick, the guy in charge of security. It felt good to be back on my game again.

The four of us were joined by Florian for dinner. He is Romanian and was hired to act as our interpreter for the trip, even though most of the locals speak excellent English. We ate at a local Romanian restaurant called Haul-Manuc. It was in the courtyard of a very old and very large building that formed the four sides of a courtyard with wooden balconies that ran on several levels completely around.

The food was good—roasted pork, which they called pastrami, and polenta. The wine was even better. Florian talked about our trip, but because James was the detail guy, I only half-listened. Instead, I took in the people of Bucharest, from the violin players entertaining us, the wait staff, the chefs, down to the patrons.

I was surprised that the Romanian NOMARs were so handsome. I had always been a guy attracted to Americans — mostly because I like them rugged and full of confidence. But these Romanians were holding their own. Many of the men had great biceps and well-defined chests that they showed off under tight t-shirts. They fell behind in the leg department, most of them choosing not to work on them in the gym, but overall, they were attractive and mysterious. I like that a lot.

Nick wanted another go after dinner, so I let him fuck me doggy-style while I watched the big hunk lose his shit deep inside me from the giant bedroom mirror. He really is a nice man and a good fuck, but I still went back to my own room to sleep.

I planned on joining the others in the morning like James had instructed.

Worried that I was going to be late, I was relieved to see that I was the second to arrive when I stepped into the hotel hallway. Roger was leaning up against his door with his face already buried in his tablet.

"Morning," I said as I closed my door and looked for a place to prop.

"Morning," he answered without looking up. A few seconds later, he asked, "Where's Nick? You wear him out last night?"

"Excuse me?" I asked in shock.

Roger finally looked up at me. "You played with the bull, and I suppose that you got the horn . . . probably several times, didn't you?"

"It's none of your damn business," I snapped as Nick's door opened and he emerged all in black again. I gave him a withering look and asked, "How do you even know, Roger?"

Roger looked back to his tablet with no concern at all. "I tapped into the hotel security feeds last night. Saw you go into Nick's room and leave an hour later. I just figured it was a good-night fuck. Was I wrong?"

Nick was watching me with an expression between surprise and humor on his face. "No, you're not wrong. He fucked the shit out of me, and I slept like a baby. You got a problem with that?"

"Nope," Roger said as he held up his hand and high-fived Nick.

"Where's James?" I snapped.

Roger answered me, "He's skipping breakfast . . . not feeling well." When we looked at him questioningly, he said, "He sent me an email."

"Let's go," Nick said, now in charge.

Breakfast was good—croissants with jam, eggs, fruit, cheeses, potatoes, and really strong coffee. I chose to have a latte and sweetened it at the table as Roger and Nick ate heartily. I was never a breakfast guy, so the coffee was my main target. Nick and my extracurricular activities had made me hungry, so I ate a croissant with cheese and some fruit. I would eat something bigger at lunch.

Roger got another email from James while we were eating. "He thinks he might have food poisoning," Roger informed us nonchalantly.

"From last night?" I asked.

"I guess," Roger said.

"I ate the same thing he did," I said worriedly.

"You would have been sick already if you were going to be," Nick informed me.

"What do we do now?" I asked the table.

Roger looked at his tablet, shoveled some muesli into his mouth and said, "He wants us to take the train to Sinaia without him, and he will catch up to us in the afternoon."

"Should we take him to a hospital or something before we leave?" I asked, thinking of how it would feel for me to be left behind sick in a foreign country.

"He's already had the hotel call for a doctor, according to

his email."

I was annoyed with this man already, and when I spoke next, it was obvious. "Do you think you can give us all the news at one time, Roger?"

He looked up at me and said, "You chose to give your ass only to some of us, so I can do the same thing with my information if I want to."

"Fuck you," I hissed as I got up from the table and left. My bags were already packed, so I returned to my room and retrieved them. I stopped long enough to write James a get-better-soon note on hotel stationery and slid it under his door.

I waited for Nick and Roger in the lobby with my bags. A taxi took us to the train station where we met Florian. Thank God, he was there, because the woman at the ticket counter did not speak English, and she did not care to even try to understand. We only knew this because a poor Indian man was right in front of us in line, and he was having a terrible time trying to get her to understand what he was saying to her in English.

Florian stepped in and translated for the Indian man and also for us. He handed us tickets for the train and indicated which way to go in the grand building that served as the station. I stopped and bought a bottle of pop for the trip and got a bottle of water for Nick. Roger could fuck himself. I was still mad at him.

Once on the right train, we waited for a few minutes before it departed and then settled in to see the countryside. The train station had been very European to me, and I was excited to see the rest of the countryside. I took the opportunity to start a conversation with the train porter, who sat with us, and he pointed to different points of interests out the windows. His English was decent, and I enjoyed meeting him.

The train soon stopped at the foothills of the Carpathian Mountains at a beautiful little town called Sinaia.

"You have to see Pelles Castle while you are here," Florian told us.

"Maybe after our meetings," I told him. With James out of the picture, I was in charge of the diplomacy and meetings. I should have looked over the paperwork on the train, but I was too interested in seeing the sites. I mainly just had to stall until the afternoon when James would join us.

Nick was taking up the slack from James' absence by taking over the logistics. He got us off the train and into a cab with no problems. I showed the driver the address of the hotel and then asked him if he could wait and take us to the first company where we had a meeting. He nodded that he could, and we were off.

Sinaia was even more beautiful than Bucharest, with cute chalets gleaming in the bright sunshine behind beautifully manicured lawns. The taxi headed into the old section of the city near the palace and stopped in front of a lovely little hotel painted a cheery yellow with white shutters.

The manager, Mihael, was very excited to have us as guests and settled us into our rooms very quickly so the cab wouldn't charge us extra. He shooed us out to the cab as soon as our luggage was dropped in the rooms.

I showed the cabbie the address for BAYtech, and he nodded his head. Turning the cab into traffic, he aimed it at the mountains, and we were soon climbing.

The company was located on a beautiful meadow at the edge of a great forest. It was securely surrounded by an imposing fencing that somehow artistically did not detract from the beauty of the location. The building itself looked ultra-modern and new. It was neither the old European romance style of architecture nor the utilitarian style of the Communists that we had only seen here.

We were stopped at the guard gate, and the cab was forced to unload and exit. We paid the cab and showed our passports to the guard, who checked a clipboard he had inside the gate.

"Wait here," he ordered in English.

Soon, a large golf cart came down the drive from the building, and the gate opened. The cart stopped, and a handsome man in his twenties got out of the driver's seat. He shook each one of our hands with a huge grin on his face and introduced himself as Alexi, assistant to the chief of development.

We were soon loaded onto the cart and heading into the building. Alexi explained that BAYtech was a technology company that specialized in sound tech. He ushered us to a conference room and brought in a big tray of coffee for us. The BAYtech team immediately joined us, and my jaw promptly hit the conference room table.

Their team was composed of three members, each one more attractive than the other. They were stunningly handsome. The head guy, Stefan, was in his thirties, and his two assistants were in their twenties. Stefan was tall with dark hair slicked back over shaved sides, which I had already seen was the Romanian style. He had dark eyes that were constantly watching and seemed very brash. Lucian, one of the assistants, was losing his hair, so it was cut short. He had a full blond beard and mustache under beautiful blue eyes. Fane also had his head shaved except the top, which was very long. He had slickly pulled it back into a very small ponytail that hung above his shaved head at the back. He had brown facial hair and warm chocolate eyes that were at once arresting and welcoming.

"Gentlemen, we are so happy to have you here at BAYtech," Stefan greeted us.

We stood and shook each of their hands as he introduced his team. I introduced our team, and we all had a seat. Stefan explained that Fane and Lucian did not speak English, so I asked Florian to interpret for them.

"There will be no need," Stefan said. "We have developed a translation app for your cell phone. They will simply plug in to understand." He said something in Romanian, and the two men took out their cells and installed one earbud in one of their ears.

"Now, we are ready, yes?" Stefan asked.

"Yes," I answered.

He looked at me for a moment and then said, "Pardon my hesitation, but it is highly unusual for a marked man to be in your position, no?"

"I guess," I said with a slight shrug. "To be honest, I wasn't expecting to be in this position, but the head of our delegation is . . . under the weather."

"Yes, Mr. High seems to have gotten a bad piece of pastrami."

How the hell does he know that?

Almost as if he could read my mind, he answered my question by saying, "Romania is a small country, no?"

"Beautiful country. We are really enjoying our trip so far.

"Excellent. Well, let's get down to business, shall we?"

"Yes," I agreed.

ABOUT THE AUTHOR

Crawford Rhine completed his first book, Batting Cage, after suddenly re-discovering the passion for writing that he had while in school. Spending each summer at the beach, he dreams of autumns in the mountains of Western Pennsylvania and winters on the slopes of Austria.

Crawford has seven books published in the Master & Servant Series, Batting Cage, Gridiron Cage, Celluloid Cage, Hardwood Cage, Ice Cage, Country Cage, and Comic-Lined Cage.

Crawford has recently finished a soon to be published new series based on classic movie monsters called The Romanian Chronicles. The first installment is titled The Dark Master and the second is titled the Reanimated Master.